WHAT

a
Friend

The Sack

Betty H. Marshall

authorHOUSE®

AuthorHouse™ LLC
1663 Liberty Drive
Bloomington, IN 47403
www.authorhouse.com
Phone: 1-800-839-8640

Published by AuthorHouse 06/16/2014

ISBN: 978-1-4969-1768-3 (sc)
ISBN: 978-1-4969-1767-6 (e)

Prologue

M AMA GREW UP dirt poor on a farm where her daddy was the last of the sharecroppers in Alabama. She only had a sixth grade education. Mama, like most young girls on farms in the rural south, ended up pregnant by local boys from neighboring farms. She had her first child at age 14 and her second child at 18. Beatrice Lela Card left Alabama and headed to Atlanta where her older sisters had migrated.

Times were extremely hard. Bea left her two children in Alabama with her Papa (father). When mama arrived in Madison County, Georgia she found it difficult to meet someone willing and worthy of marrying. However, when a woman has two children, very little education, and no viable means of support husbands don't come knocking at your door. Therefore, mama did what her sisters before her had done. She became a domestic worker.

The money was minimal but it was more than mama had ever had before. Mama was living with her sister and relying on cabs to take her everywhere she had to go. Bea met a cab driver and they became friendly. With the encouragement of her sister mama married the man. Clarence (Dial) Harris was much older than mama and had no real means of support except taxi driving. He also had another life that mama didn't come to know about until years later.

Dedication

To: BRANNETTE LEOLA, Richard Earl, Richard, Nyaisha, Rhiantae, Mary Ann, Larita Denise, Ornie Lee, Terrence Maurice, Cheyne, Sheridan, Chante, Nita, Bet, Kay, Sam, Deborah, Pamela, Thomas, James P., Sharon, Thomas, James Dallas, Robert Lee, Rachel, Jamya, Remya. Sw, To my Aunt Bell, Cathalean, and my parents, Leola and Clarence who have all gone on to be with the Lord. May they rest in peace.

I love you all,
Bjhm

PART I

Chapter 1

I T WAS EARLY Saturday morning. I woke up with my white cotton nightgown stuck to my small brown frame. I went into mama and daddy's room. I looked at the big bed that mama and daddy shared and saw that mama and daddy were already up. I ran to the back door and saw daddy shaving and Mama was hanging out the wash. I went back to the sink, washed my face, and brushed my teeth.

It was already 80 degrees and it seemed like steam was rising from the concrete. My daddy would always walk out on the back porch and say "its gon be so hot you can fry an egg on that concrete". I always wanted to fry an egg on that concrete but mama would never give me an egg. She said eggs were too hard to come by. After I got grown, and had to buy my own eggs I figured out what mama meant by eggs being hard to come by.

I was sitting under the wet sheets and handing Mama clothespins when her mouth got empty of the two she was holding between her lips and two front teeth. "Hand me another clothes pin baby and come from under the sheets before you get something on them." Mama said in her sweet southern drawl. The mud that was made from the water dripping from the wet clothes was cool between my fat toes.

I had run out of the house so fast that morning I had forgotten my flip-flops. The pin that I had put in the big toe of my flip-flops had twisted and caused a sore spot to develop between my big toe and my first toe.

Mama was little, but powerfully built. She had a nice frame that stayed lean from hard work. She had lived on a farm in Alabama and was the last of thirteen children. She was the baby of the family.

Mama was no stranger to hard work. Her daddy had been a sharecropper and she and her brothers and sisters picked cotton until their backs hurt and their fingers bled. Mama said she would work night and day to keep her children from that kind of hard labor.

When mama looked down and saw my feet and hands covered with thick reddish brown mud she threatened me with a whipping that I would never forget. Mama didn't whip me because she had a soft heart, and a soft spot for me and for all of her children. However, she could make you feel lower than a toad on a lily pad just by giving you one of her soulful you hurt me looks when you did something wrong. Of course with three children in the house things were bound to go wrong most of the time.

Mama finished hanging out the wash. I went to the side of the house and washed my feet in the rain bucket under the shed. Bessie the tabby cat was lying on her side licking her fur. Mama came around the side of the house and flung the wash water out before she looked. Bessie and I got soaked. Bessie took out running and I just stood there dripping wet. The water felt good to my body because it was ten o'clock in the morning and the heat was sweltering. "Lord." mama cooed. "I didn't see my angel there. Mama didn't mean it. C'mon let's get you dried off and comb your hair." she said. I got dried off and pulled another cotton sheath over my little brown frame. Mama sent me to get the two milk crates from the back room to sit on to get my hair braided. My hair was thick and wooly and there was nothing I hated more than to get my hair pressed and combed. Mama would take the comb and lay it close to my head to pick up what she called the little b b shots. I sat there and endured that agony for 30 minutes twice a week, and once on Sunday morning before church.

Every night I had to tie a headscarf around my head to keep my hair in place for school the next day. If you didn't keep your hair nice everybody called you nappy headed.

My brother, who is next to me, had a bottle route. His name was Willie Earl Harris. He was named after mama's brother in Alabama. He collected glass bottles and sold them for two cents each. He would canvas the neighborhood with his red radio flyer wagon. It had been rebuilt with wooden slats that he, my big brother, and my daddy had found at the dumpsite at the edge of town. He would make a lot of money especially in the summer time just from hanging around the city barbershop. Sometimes he would let me go with him. Most of the time he would say, "I don't want a nappy headed baby girl hanging around me. It slows up my business." Mama would say, "you watch yourself little man you talking bigger than them britches you wearing and if I say she go with you then she go with you. Now you go on about your business before I send her with you." My brother would go on off with his head up in the air and mumbling to himself like he was a real big time businessman.

Willie Earl would come home with all of the news from town. Mama would always say "don't you bring that street gossip in my house." She and daddy would pretend not to listen. But I would always hear mama telling my auntie what my brother had said, and telling her not to tell anybody, but she always told everybody at church, choir rehearsal, and prayer meeting. She even told Sister Viola who was supposed to lead the church in the Holy Ghost dance on Sunday mornings. If Miss Viola didn't get the Holy Ghost nobody else was supposed to get it.

Miss Viola had a son that looked almost white. His lips let you know that he wasn't all the way white because they were full and round. His hair was curly and black, and he had gray eyes. He was around the same age as Willie. Miss Viola didn't let him play with the rest of us. He went to school across town. His clothes were different too. Folks wondered where Miss Viola got the money to dress him like that, and send him across town to the Colored Training School. Mama said, "It wasn't for us to know and to mind our own business."

My brother was our lifeline to the outside world. He even knew the white folks business. He would go to pick up

Miss Francine's wash every Monday morning before school and he would take his time putting it in the Croaker sack mama had given him so he could bring it back home.

Miss Francine Rooker was the mayor's wife and folks said she got her clothes from the Sears Roebuck catalog, and they brought the clothes directly to her house. Miss Francine would have her ladies group in on Monday mornings at 7am for breakfast before it got to hot. Hattie Mae Reynolds said she wasn't cooking breakfast for nobody, black or white after7: o'clock. Hattie meant every word she said. Miss Hattie was Miss Francine's cook and housekeeper. Nobody wanted to get on Miss Hattie's bad side because when she got mad all of Madison County knew it. Folks say Miss Hattie had killed a woman one time that was messing around with her husband. She had cut the woman's head off and put it in a pillowcase and threw it on the train tracks. Of course nobody could prove it, and nobody dared bring it up for fear of Miss Hattie cutting his or her head off.

Willie Earl would stay in the shed putting clothes in the sack and listening to everything they said and bringing the wash, and the gossip home to our little house on Merritt Street.

Mama was known throughout the county for her washing and ironing ability. After all nobody could press and starch a shirt like mama. White folks always teased mama and said "Bea Harris could starch and press the neck of a shirt so stiff that a man dare not turn his head too fast or far unless he wanted to pick up his goose pipe off the hot Georgia concrete."

My oldest brother Sammy (Samuel Micah Harris) was named after somebody in the bible. He was the coolest one in our family. He was a senior at the all black Booker Taliaferro Washington high school. He was a football hero and a track star. He was tall broad shouldered and good looking. All the girls were crazy about Sammy. He was over six feet tall with smooth dark skin and big brown eyes. Sammy always wore a tie and shirt to school. He wore his hair low and close to his head with a nice part on the right side of his head. All of our neighbors talked about how polite Sammy was, and how hard he worked at everything he did. When the rich white folks had a party they always asked for Sammy to work for them. Not in the kitchen with the others but out front handing folks little sandwiches and bubbling drinks. Sometimes Sammy would bring home the leftover sandwiches that the people he worked for gave him. They had strange fillings inside of them. They had funny little pieces of bread with no crust. Sammy said they were called "Lady Fingers". He was right because they were hardly bigger than a finger. But they were good. Mama would always say how it was a shame how folks wasted bread, and people hungry right here on Merritt Street. But mama was that way always worrying about other folks.

One Sunday afternoon we were all sitting on the front porch, except Sammy. He was allowed to visit Mary Lynn Philpot, (everybody called her Pearline) on Sunday evenings if all of his chores were done, and he didn't have an early ball practice the next morning.

My brother Willie Earl was turning the crank on the ice cream freezer as fast and as hard as he could and the ice cream was just about right for adding the berries me and mama had picked that morning. Everybody in Madison County knew that you had to do your berry picking before the 11 o'clock sun got past the tall magnolia trees, and burned you to a crisp. I learned that lesson the hard way.

One morning mama and daddy had gone down to the Curb market to get some greens and chitterlings for the rent party they were throwing that night for the Johnson family that lived 6 streets over from our house. My best friend Lola was the youngest girl in the Johnson family and one of the prettiest girls I knew.

Lola's daddy had gotten laid off from the Fulton Madison County Feed and Bag factory, and they didn't have the $22.00 for the rent. Lola had been my best friend since kindergarten. One day when we were at school and we had gone out for recess I was busy playing a game of Red Light and it was my turn to be it. The teacher called us from the recess yard to go use it. I didn't stop to go to the restroom so I wet my clothes. Lola gave me her sweater to tie around me so that no one could see my wet clothes. When we left the playground to line up and be dismissed to go home Lola stayed close behind me just in case someone might see something. But Lola's long sweater covered my whole bottom completely. She has been my best friend every since.

Lola was tall and slim. She had thick braids that twirled around her head like cotton candy. When we would run and play and get real sweaty the braids would come undone and her hair would become curlier and twice as thick. She was a dark chocolate with big white teeth that seemed to light up a room. When Lola would spend the night with me we would sleep under the bed and Lola's teeth were so white they seemed to glow in the dark room. We didn't even need a flashlight to read the comic books we had sneaked from my brother's treasure box. There were so many things in that treasures box that Lola and I didn't understand until we got older.

One afternoon we (Lola and I) got it into our heads to go berry picking after 11:30. We went to pick berries and the sun was so strong on my skin that it felt like someone was ironing my clothes right onto my back. When we got back to the house mama was waiting on the porch with a switch. When she saw the burn on my back she said "looks to me like you already got a good whipping from the sun". Lola and I went into the house and mama covered our backs with a mayonnaise paste she had made. She would sometimes use that same paste on Daddy and my brothers when they had worked in the hot sun all day. The plaster felt good on our scorched skin. Mama made us lay down in the cool dark smoke house the rest of the afternoon or at least until our backs cooled down. Lola's teeth glowed in the dark smoke house.

The ham hanging from the hook looked like a monster as it cast a shadow across the room and Lola's teeth didn't make things any better. They glowed so brightly that they caused the scary shadow to radiate from the big old ham hanging from the hook on the wall.

As we sat there on the porch churning the ice cream two white men dressed in dark suits walked up on our porch. They looked scary. They talked directly to my daddy calling him Mr. Harris. I had never seen white men up that close before, and that spoke nicely to my daddy. The taller one had a briefcase with lots of papers inside. He reminded me of Miss Francine's husband except Mr. Rooker's hair was white and had a bald spot in the middle. Mr. Rooker always combed his hair from the sides to cover his bald spot on top as if people wouldn't know that the bald spot was there. People knew because my brother Willie Earl told us that the men in the barber shop always laughed at Mr. Rooker and said that Miss Francine had worried his hair right off his head with her high falooting ways and big spending. She was always buying those clothes out of the Sears Roebuck catalog and having them brought right to her front door by the postman.

Willie Earl said that he had seen Miss Francine give the Postman a one-dollar bill for bringing the packages to her house, and invite him in the house for iced tea. Willie Earl also said that Mr. Rooker had come home early one day from downtown and caught the Postman at the house.

Mr. Rooker was the mayor and the funeral home director. The people of Madison County had converted the back of Rooker's funeral home into the mayor's office and decorated it with brown parchment paper and Japanese lanterns. Some folks said it looked more like a New Orleans brothel than a mayor's office/funeral home. I didn't know what a New Orleans brothel looked like so I asked my brother Willie Earl what it was. He said it was a hotel for fast ladies. Well I still didn't know. Willie Earl said I needed to be quiet and go play with Lola or somebody because he was too busy to tell me. Willie Earl's face looked funny and he started to sweat. He yelled at me to "go". It scared me so I ran and hid under the house in my secret place. It was where Lola and me played with our dolls.

Mr. Rooker had come home early one day and found the post man sitting on the settee from Sears Roebuck and ran the post man out into the street and threw his packages out behind him, and Miss Francine had screamed so loudly that the paddy wagon had come. Mr. Rooker had to do some smooth talking to keep them from taking both of them downtown for what Willie Earl called "disturbed peace." I never knew what that meant until years later when daddy had to go downtown for the same thing. Daddy had gotten into an argument with the man who drove the ice wagon. Daddy said that he had overcharged him for his ice. Daddy and the iceman got into a tussle and mama and our neighbor threw cold water on them to separate them. Daddy couldn't talk his way out of it like Mr. Rooker. Daddy had to spend 3 days downtown for the "disturbed peace" and mama had to pay ten dollars for daddy to come home. We ate fatback and rice for a whole month after that deal.

The tall man made our porch seem dwarf like with his tall wide frame and broad shoulders. He pulled papers out of the brown case and gave them to my daddy one at a time. He explained each paper to him and talked to my daddy like he was a man like him. Both of the men turned and spoke politely to my mother. I didn't understand all that they were saying but I remember words like scholarship, and all-star, and academics. I finally figured out that they were talking about my big brother Sammy.

The shorter man said that they wanted to give my brother a scholarship. They explained to my daddy that a scholarship was free money, room and board to go to their school if he (Sammy) played football for them.

Mama got so excited that the berries we had spent all morning picking suddenly scattered and rolled from her lap onto the plank porch and through the cracks onto the dirt underneath.

I scrambled to try and save as many berries as I could but daddy said it was time for Willie Earl and me to go into the house and get ready for bed. Well needless to say there was no ice cream to be eaten that night.

I went to bed wondering about scholarships and longing for some ice cream to cool my parched tongue and throat.

Lola came early the next morning for school. Willie Earl had already gone to pick up the wash from Miss Francine's house and Sammy had left early for practice. Lola waited on the steps for me to come out.

Mama had packed two lunches because Lola never had any food at her house. She had so many brothers and a sister that I think they had to take turns eating. Mama said Lola probably ate like a bird at her house so that her brothers and sisters could have enough. I knew for a fact that Lola did not eat like a bird. She ate like a horse. She was skinny because she spent so much time running through the streets to our house to eat. Lola was my best friend.

We were late again and had to run most of the last eight blocks to get to school before the bell rang. We were always late because my hair had to be combed fresh on the mornings that my head rag had come undone and slipped off my head. I would wake up with the rag halfway between the top of my head and my throat. I remember waking up one morning with what felt like a noose around my neck. The head rag was choking me to death. I vowed never to wear it again. Mama said I had to wear it or wake up with a nappy head. I resorted to wearing the rag around my head to kiss mama and daddy good night. Then as soon as I got in the bed I would take the rag off and stuff it under my pillow. This behavior resulted in a nappy head the next morning, which took an extra ten minutes to fix. Therefore, we were always rushing so that we would not be late for school.

This particular morning we were running extra late because my hair would not lay down on my head no matter how much grease mama put on it. She finally took some bobby pins and stuck my big fat braids to my head.

We decided to take a short cut through the alley behind the beauty shop. We would sometimes see Miss Francine in there with some things stuck to her head that looked like aluminum foil wrapped around a clothes hanger. I would stand on the crates we found in the alley to see into the beauty shop. Lola was tall enough to see inside without any help if she stood on her tippy toes, and stretched her neck up high.

We rushed through the alley that morning not taking time for a peek in the Beeline Beauty Parlor or anything else. All of a sudden Big Frank came out of nowhere. He grabbed us by our arms and flung us to the ground. Lola kicked and scratched at Big Frank. I started to cry. Big Frank laughed and his rotten teeth gleamed through his thick black lips. He seemed to enjoy our struggle and our tears. The more we struggled the harder and tighter his grip on our arms. Lola screamed and Big Frank slapped her across the face and yelled at her to shut up.

When Lola fell to the ground she screamed, "Run Pookie run!" I was frozen in my tracks. I couldn't run. I couldn't scream. I just stood there frozen. Big Frank lunged at me and that's when I found my feet. I ran as fast as I could and I didn't stop until I was inside of the big schoolhouse doors.

Lola didn't come to school that day or the next day. When I got home at the end of the week I went straight to the Johnson house and knocked on Lola's back door. Her sister came to the door and said Lola couldn't come out to play, and that I couldn't come over anymore. Lola was my best friend.

I replayed the scene over and over in my head all day long. I wanted to tell mama what happened but I was afraid she would whip me. We had been warned to stay away from that alley. Even though we were late for school mama would still have been mad. Lola was my best friend.

Nobody in Madison County could stand Big Frank. Folks said he was crazy in his head. Folks said it wasn't his fault. They said Big Frank was born that way. Willie Earl had told us that he had heard folks talking about Frank in the Big Sun grocery store in town. They said that his mama was a drinking woman who didn't know who Big Frank's daddy was. I told Willie Earl that I didn't understand how you couldn't know who your daddy was and Willie Earl said that "I was slow in the head," and he went on collecting his bottles, and I went in the back door and let the screen door slam real hard. I was mad and I didn't care who knew it. Lola was my best friend.

Sammy was busy rushing around in his bedroom. He was packing things in a trunk big enough for me to lie down in if I scrunched myself up into a tight ball. Mama came in with a hand full of freshly starched shirts and pants. "Here" mama said. That ought to hold you until you can get back here for Christmas."

Sammy packed the shirts into one of the other bags that were already overflowing with books and supplies that all the church folk had given him last Sunday at the BTU services. The pastor had talked on and on about Sammy and how he had worked so hard with the Baptist Training Union at our church.

Some of the men in the church had prayed over Sammy and laid hands on his head and anointed him with the oil from Miss Viola's purse. Some folks said that it was nothing but Crisco lard that Miss Viola had saved from the chicken she fried every Sunday.

Sammy's girlfriend had cried along with Mama and Daddy. I didn't cry. I was still mad. Now I had two things to be mad over. As I was leaving the church I thought that

I saw Lola out of the corner of my eye sitting on the stump across the street in the vacant lot. When I turned around to get a good look I didn't see her. I figured my mind was playing tricks on me. Life was changing in Madison County and me along with it.

Chapter 2

THE TRAIN PULLED into the station at exactly 11:15 Saturday morning. Sammy was standing on the platform and my daddy was standing directly to his right and mama on his left. Willie Earl and I were standing in front of them all. Mama's other two children had come up from the country to see Sammy off. We didn't spend a whole lot of time together but when we did on holidays and special occasions it was as if we were never apart. They didn't want to come and stay with us even though mama and daddy had offered many times.

Maurva Jean had her own life and had graduated from high school and worked in a book keeping office. Bailey was helping mama's daddy with the farm and wanted to have his own farm some day. They loved Sammy and wanted to be with him on his big day along with the rest of Madison County.

The mayor had said that Sammy was a real credit to his race and he would do well and represent Madison County in a real special way. Miss Francine had her hair done just to see Sammy off to college, and she was wearing her new dress from the Sears Roebuck catalog. She had showed the picture in the catalog to anyone that would look when she was in the Madison County drugstore at the lunch counter.

A man from the Madison county Herald newspaper took a picture of our family and told my daddy he could come by about the middle of next week and see the proofs. Daddy gave him a twenty-five cent deposit. The man gave daddy a card with his name and the address of his office printed on the front and a flag on the back of it. It was the same flag that was in my classroom hanging next to the United States flag. It had a big red x on it and the rest of it was white. I had seen that flag being carried by some boys in the back of a pick-up truck going down our street one night. Just before daddy made us all go down in the root cellar in the smoke house I saw big flames of fire and heard what sounded like screams coming from our neighbor's house across the street.

Mr. Robert Griffin had lived in that house as long as I could remember. When his sister came down from Detroit to live with him after her husband had died people did not talk to Mr. Robert Griffin anymore. Everybody crossed the street and mama told us to never go to that house again.

Mr. Griffin's sister looked white. She had long straight hair and green eyes. I heard mama tell Miss Hattie that Mr. Robert Griffin had death on him, and it was just a matter of time before it happened. I didn't know what that meant but the next day after we saw the flames at that house I found out. Daddy, Willie Earl, and Sammy left the root cellar early that morning. Daddy told me and mama to stayed in that root cellar until he came back and told us to come out. Willie Earl told me later that some men in white hoods and robes had killed Mr. Robert Griffin.

They had put a rope around his neck and hanged him from the tree in his front yard. Then they poured gasoline on him and set him on fire. Mr. Rooker's funeral home men came and took Mr. Robert Griffin's sister away. Willie Earl said that daddy and some more men had taken Mr. Robert Griffin's body down and buried it in the field behind his house. They couldn't take him to the church because the men had threatened to kill them if they saw them with the body in town.

Willie Earl held me tight and we cried together for what Willie had seen and what I had imagined in my mind.

Mama was holding on tight to Sammy like she wasn't sure she would ever see him again. Willie Earl went off looking for bottles and gossip. Many of the people from Madison County had heard about Sammy's scholarship and had come to see him off. The mayor and Miss Francine, Miss Viola, Miss Hattie, Coach Solomon from the high school had come with the two white men that had come to our house that Sunday afternoon with the news of the scholarship, Auntie Chauncey, the pastor, and several men from the BTU that Sammy worked with at church, and Sammy's girlfriend Pearline. Sammy had told Pearline that he was going to come back and marry her. I heard him tell her that on the back porch one hot night when I was supposed to be in bed asleep but chose to stay on the porch in the hammock. They never knew I was there. He had kissed Pearline real hard that night. I was looking straight at him through the holes in the hammock.

I thought that I caught a glimpse of Lola peeking through the hedges at the corner of the station but when I went to look I didn't see her. My mind was always playing tricks on me when it came to Lola.

Sammy finally got on the train. The porters helped him load his trunk and showed him to his seat. We waved the train out of sight. We went home and mama made a dinner of tuna fish sandwiches and kool aide. It was my favorite Saturday dinner but I couldn't eat. Mama sat there staring out into space, and daddy finally got up and said he was going into town for some tobacco.

I went outside looking for Bessie. She was sunning herself on the porch as usual. She came over to me and rubbed against my leg. It was as if she could sense my sadness.

The air hung thick over the house on Merritt Street like a fog on a rainy morning. It was beginning to get chilly in the mornings. October had turned into November and leaves were everywhere. I walked to school that morning and kicked the leaves that surrounded my ankles. They were a beautiful gold, orange, and brown and crunched under my feet as I walked along. I darted across the street as I approached the Beeline Beauty shop. I rounded the corner and walked straight into Lola. I gasped and reached my arms out to her. As I reached for her she vanished. Was my mind playing tricks on me or was she really there. Lola was my best friend and I missed her terribly.

Daddy had become attached to the radio. Every Saturday afternoon he would sit on the front porch and listen to the football announcer call out the ball player's names. He did not hear Sammy's name that whole season. Needless to say Daddy was puzzled and vexed by the whole thing. He kept listening every Saturday anyway.

I woke up early one morning and looked out of the window. It was a cold and frosty December morning. I thought that I was seeing things. It was Sammy standing on the porch. I jumped out of bed and ran through the house yelling, "It's Sammy. It's Sammy!" Daddy came from the kitchen with a half-shaven face. It was winter and daddy shaved in the house in the kitchen during the winter. He looked at me with a puzzled expression on his face. Then he looked past me and he saw what I was screaming about. Mama came from the bedroom pulling on her housecoat and she and daddy saw what I was screaming about at the same time. Willie Earl stumbled in from the room he and Sammy had shared just a few months before. Everyone rushed towards Sammy and hugged him. Once again it was happy times in the house on Merritt Street.

It was two weeks before Christmas and mama and daddy had just brought in the Christmas tree. It was a beautiful tree that daddy had cut himself from the Georgia woods. All of the decorations that we hung on our tree were hand made by the family. Willie Earl had made several funny little Santa's from wood and string and bottle caps that he had collected. One year while Sammy was still in high school, he was taking a shop class, and he carved a Mary and Joseph manager scene and several other little ornaments. While I was in the Ladies Aide and Girls Missionary Society at church I had crocheted, and knitted several ornaments. We had shipped many of the homemade items like scarves and mittens overseas to people in foreign countries.

We took pride in hanging the ornaments on our tree every year. Mama always made Lane Cakes that we kids were not even allowed to sniff let alone taste. I didn't taste a Lane cake until I had graduated from high school. She made coconut cakes, chocolate cakes, and sweet potato pies. The pastor always got a coconut cake for Christmas, and his wife got a chocolate cake. Mama always made a special fuss over the cakes she made for them. She would make the icing thicker, and the layers fluffier.

The pastor and his wife would stop by and pick up the cakes and have special prayer to bless our house for the holidays and the New Year. Our cousins, Johnnie Mae, and Estelle, and my uncle George and Auntie Lula Pope, all came to our house during the Christmas. My cousin Johnnie Mae always peed in the bed. I would try to stop her from drinking too much kool-aide but she wouldn't listen. She would drink three cups and then she would go to sleep and pee on me and the pallet, that mama had made for us to sleep on. Johnnie Mae would sleep right through the wetness while I got soaking wet from her kool-aide pee induced deep sleep.

One night during the Christmas my uncle George went with mama and daddy to the Johnson's for a Christmas party. George drank lots of Lola's daddy's special punch. I knew that punch was special because one day Lola and I came home from playing with our friends in the neighborhood and saw the tub her daddy made the punch in and we drank a pitcher full. I tried to walk home but I fell down over and over again. Everything was spinning around and around. I fell asleep as soon as I got home. I didn't wake up until the next morning. My head was hurting and spinning at the same time. I am glad that mama thought that I had a virus. She didn't know that we had drunk Lola's daddy's special punch the day before.

That night while everyone was asleep my Uncle George got up and started to eat the dinner that mama had made for the next day. Uncle George took the ham out and bit big chunks out of it like a wild dog. He bit right out of the middle of mama's sweet potato pie, and dug a big hole out of the potato salad.

When mama woke up the next morning and saw the food she fainted right there in the middle of the kitchen floor. When mama woke up from her fainting spell she took Uncle George's clothes and suitcases and threw them in the yard. She told them all to get out and not come back. Auntie Lula, and the children all left and we did not see them again for a long time. Mama said some words that I had never heard before. My head was hurting and spinning at the same time, and all the yelling and running around made it feel like it was going to pop off of my body. I am glad that mama thought that I had a virus. She didn't know that we had drunk Lola's daddy's special punch the day before.

While Sammy was home for the holidays I was always late for school. Mama fixed a big breakfast and we sat around and talked. Sammy explained to my daddy that none of the new boys got to play the first season. They were "red shirted," and that was why we hadn't heard his name on the radio. I often thought about Sammy wearing a red shirt and it didn't seem right to make him or any of the new boys wear red shirts. Red didn't even look good on my big brother.

Willie Earl forgot to pick up Miss Francine's wash that morning and she sent her yardman with it to our house. He told mama that Miss Francine had pitched a fit because Mr. Rooker needed his shirts that night for the special Christmas Program downtown. She said, "she could get her another woman to do her laundry if Miss Bea didn't shape up". Needless to say mama was madder than a hornet. As she walked into her bedroom it sounded like mama said something about Miss Francine shoving her laundry somewhere. I couldn't understand all of it but I knew mama was mad by the way she slammed her bedroom door.

I ran out of house as fast as I could. I had to get to school before the bell rang. Miss Sutton told me that if I were tardy one more day I would lose my recess. As I ran around the corner I ran smack into Lola. There was no doubt this time. It was Lola. Lola was my best friend. Lola didn't look like herself. It was something about her eyes. They looked empty and glazed over. Lola was not skinny any more she was thin. Her clothes hung on her like rags. The dress hung from under the coat she was wearing like it didn't belong on her body. The coat didn't have buttons. It had a big safety pin looped in the buttonhole. The pin didn't hold her coat together. It just hung there like an unwanted bug. Lola would not look directly at me. She turned away from me when she talked. I finally caught a glimpse of her mouth and her front tooth was missing. There was a black hole where the beautiful white tooth had once radiated from her mouth. Her hair was matted and hadn't been combed for what looked like days. When I reached out to embrace her she broke away and yelled, "Let me go". I started to cry. "Lola it's me Pookie". "Remember, Pookie". She looked at me as if I were something from a dark part of her brain.

Lola ran into the street screaming back at me, "stay away from me". I tried to run after her but I tripped and fell to my knees and cried. I cried and sobbed until I felt as if my breath was leaving my body. I suddenly felt something singe the side of my head and face. It felt like a hot poker. Everything went black. That is all that I remember.

When I woke up I didn't open my eyes. My head throbbed and my arm hurt so badly that I wanted to cry. I could hear voices in the room. Mama was talking to someone whose voice I had not heard before.

"Give her two of these tablets only if she complains about pain," the voice said. "Her arm had a clean break, and judging from the way it was broken she did not fall directly on it. She took most of the blow to her head and face. It is a good thing that the car only grazed her, and it was able to swerve around her as she fell into the street." the voice went on. The driver said, "He saw someone run away as Annie fell over. It is a good thing that she is young and strong. Those are the things in her favor, and will help her to recover quickly. She'll be good as new in a week or two. Just keep her quiet and comfortable." The voice droned on. "Yes doctor," my mother said. She thanked the doctor and I heard footsteps moving towards the back door. I fell into a fitful sleep. I had a terrible nightmare.

I woke up sweating, shaking, and screaming. Mama came running into the room. Daddy and Willie Earl were close behind. "Sammy, where is Sammy" I screamed. "Sammy went to Pearline's baby," mama said. "Tell mama what's wrong". I couldn't get it out. I sobbed so hard that my chest hurt. Mama cooed and stroked my face until I calmed down. I looked at daddy and I looked at Willie Earl. They were both dressed as if they were going out. Daddy had on his heavy coat and steel toe boots and so did Willie Earl. I saw a look pass between mama and daddy that made chills run up and down my spine. Daddy said he had to go and Willie Earl was hot on his tracks. Mama yelled for daddy but all I heard was the back door slam.

Mama sat with me and rocked me until I drifted back off into another cycle of fitful sleep and horrid dreams.

Daddy and Willie Earl met up with Lola's daddy Mr. Johnson. They walked the six blocks to Mr. John Curtis' barbershop. Mr. Curtis cut all of the black men in town hair. Willie Earl had told us that Mr. Curtis had a room in the back of his shop where all the men went after their haircuts.

They stayed a long time, and when they came out they all walked funny and had a funny smell. Willie Earl said one time when nobody was watching he peeked in that room and saw a stove with a big curvy pipe with something like water dripping through it. Before he could get a closer look someone called for him to shine their shoes.

Mr. Curtis' wife had a beauty shop right next door to the barbershop, but she only worked there on Friday afternoons and all day Saturday because she worked in Vick's Drug/ Lunch Counter cleaning up during the week.

Willie Earl said that one time he had made a dollar shining shoes and wanted to taste some food from Vick's. He had seen people coming and going from Vick's with sacks of food and the food smelled good as the people passed by his shoe shine box next to the barber shop. Willie Earl said he went into Vick's one day and the man had been real mean to him and told him to get his black ass out of there and go around back with the rest of the niggers if he wanted some food.

Willie Earl had waited a whole hour at the back of Vick's where colored people were served and ordered a hamburger with everything to go. The woman at the window gave him the hamburger in his hand, took his dollar and slammed the window shut.

Willie Earl said that he wanted the big bag with the yellow V on the front more than he wanted the hamburger. He walked back out to the street and threw the hamburger in the trash. It just wasn't the same without the bag with the big yellow V. Willie Earl sat on his shoe shine box and made little shapes with his bottle caps and bits of broken shoe laces he saved from collecting bottles and shining shoes with broken laces.

The men went in through the back door. It was dark and quiet. The only light in the room came from the moon shining through the windowpanes. Every time a car passed by they would duck down. Someone had found Sammy and told him about the meeting. The men kept the door cracked and a small fan running to keep the windows from fogging up which would give the angry group of men away to anyone passing by. Mr. Johnson spoke first. "Good evening. I know you all done heard by now about what happened to my Lola," he said in his rich baritone voice.

Some of the men cried after they heard the whole story. Mr. Johnson sang in the Male Choir at church and was always singing solos. The ladies always called on him to sing "Guide Me Ore Thou Great Jehovah". The ladies all got the Holy Ghost when Mr. Johnson sang. Mama said, "That man can't keep a job but he sure can sing." All the ladies got the Holy Ghost without Miss Viola's permission when Mr. Johnson sang.

"I would have taken matters into my own hands a long time ago." Mr. Johnson said. "But as you all know Big Frank and his family are all in good with the white folks and they leave Frank on the loose to terrorize Black folks, and keep fear running through the community." said Mr. Johnson.

"You all know that Frank always takes the money from Rooker's funeral home to the bank for old man Rooker. He also takes the money from the Big Sun to the bank. he said. Frank couldn't read or write so they trusted him with the money. Besides, they gave him $10.00 a month for his trouble. It was just enough to keep Frank drunk for a while." Mr. Johnson went on.

"I was sweeping the floors in the bank like I do every morning when Frank came in. It just so happened that Mr. Rutherford, the bank manager, was real busy that morning because it was the first of the month and folks were cashing checks and so forth. Mr. Rutherford trusted me because I work at his mama's house, his sister's house, and his house. So he asked me to see about Frank. I took the sack looked inside and saw the money and some papers. I was getting ready to put the money and the papers in the safe box when the papers fell on the floor. I read them as I picked them up. One was a paper with some real important private information on it.

Something spooked Frank. I think it was because he saw me reading what was on the paper. He snatched the sack from me and ran from the bank. I don't know why, but he just ran with the money and the sack," Curtis said. "Well we finally got it out of Lola what happened. If it hadn't been for my wife I would have gotten him myself by now," Mr. Johnson said in a voice filled with anger and hurt.

Mr. Curtis said that Big Frank had brushed up against his wife several times as she left the Big Sun where Frank worked. Several of the men in the room had reported incidences of Big Frank's inappropriate behavior. Frank had been seen peeking in the windows of houses with young girls.

He was a terror to the neighborhood and these men were willing to risk their lives and business' to put a stop to Frank once and for all. They made a plan that night and took care of Big Frank the following night when the boys were not around to witness the whipping they put on Frank for hurting a little child like Lola Johnson. They tied Frank to the pole in the back of the Beeline Beauty Shop and gave him fifty hard licks with the paddle that belonged to Coach Solomon from the high school. Needless to say Frank had a sore behind after that whipping. But the men knew that wasn't enough, Frank needed to be in jail. Some how they would see to him getting his due, they didn't know how but they would find a way.

Mama paced the floor half the night waiting for daddy and Willie Earl to return to Merritt Street. They finally came in through the back door and daddy was carrying Willie Earl over his shoulder. Mama screamed when she saw them. "Lord is my child dead? Mama yelled. "No he ain't dead" daddy said. He just wore out". Daddy took Willie's limp body in the bedroom and mama undressed him and put him in bed. The next morning daddy left and came back with a sack. Daddy turned to Sammy then and told him what to do with the sack he had flung over his back. Sammy and Willie Earl did exactly what Daddy said to do with the sack.

Chapter 3

I WOKE UP AND saw Willie Earl sitting at the foot of my bed. He looked at me and said, "You ain't sick no more. Get up right now." I had been feeling stronger. If it hadn't been for the cast on my arm everything would have been back to normal.

Willie Earl had stopped by the elementary school everyday to pick up my homework from Miss Sutton. He filled me in as best he could about what was happening in the neighborhood.

Every time I asked him about Lola he changed the subject. He told me that all the kids in the elementary school had asked about me, and Miss Sutton had sent a fruit basket, and a card that the kids in my class had made for me, and they had all signed the card and made funny pictures on the back.

Willie Earl had stuck by me all through my sickness. Mama said he told her "he didn't want me to die. Even though I was a pest and a pain in the neck I was still his baby sister, and he needed somebody to boss around, and talk to when Sammy wasn't home.

It had been Willie Earl who told me about what happened at Mr. Curtis' barbershop that night. I thought it had all been a bad dream but everything that had happened in the last two weeks was as real as anything I had ever seen. "I said get up right now!" Willie Earl said in his serious businessman's voice. I got up and tried to chase him around the room but I was still a little weak.

Mama came in and made Willie Earl leave and helped me bathe and get dressed. Mama said, the doctor told her I could go back to school in the New Year. The doctor had been good about coming by to see me. Daddy had paid him by cutting his grass and fixing his washing machine. The doctor and his wife had seven children and Lord knows they needed their washing machine. In a way it was good that I wasn't going back to school until next year because I could spend time with Sammy. The whole time he was home Sammy divided his time between our house and Pearline's house. I didn't mind. I was just happy we were all home and safe in the house on Merritt Street.

Christmas morning finally arrived. I got up and got myself dressed as best as I could. Mama came in and helped me. The cast was on my left arm, which was good because I was right handed. At least that allowed me to do some things without help. We always went to church before anything else on Christmas morning. We didn't even eat until we came back from church. We walked the four blocks and met up with neighbors on the way. Every one exchanged Christmas greetings. Everyone hugged me and told me how well I looked and how nicely my face was healing and you could hardly see the scars at all. Mama had rubbed all of my scars with a homemade paste the whole time I was sick. I had lost so much weight that my clothes hung off my body. I walked down the street and wondered where Lola was.

I was standing in the front room waiting for Sammy. He was leaving on the 11:15 train again. I was sad that he was leaving but I was glad he was going back to school. I had made him a special going away present with mama's help while I was convalescing from my accident. Sammy came in and picked me up like he always did and hugged me gently so as not to hurt the cast on my arm. "I am going to miss my baby sister." He said. He put me down and walked out of the front door. This time only daddy went to the train depot with Sammy. Mama said it was easier on all of us that way.

Daddy came back just in time for lunch. The look on his face was one that I had never seen before. Mama sat down and Willie Earl rushed through the back door with the news that changed our world and the house on Merritt Street permanently.

When Willie Earl came through the kitchen door he was breathing so hard it seemed like his chest was going to burst open. His coat was rising and falling like the pump on the well in the backyard. His forehead glistened with sweat and his hands were trembling. "Daddy, Daddy! " Willie Earl shouted. You won't believe what happened. "Slow down boy; catch your breath," daddy said as he pulled out a chair for Willie Earl to sit down. "Bea, will you get Willie Earl some water so that he can cool down?" Daddy asked. Mama brought the glass of water and a cool rag for Willie Earl's head. "Daddy I don't think Pookie should hear this and mama neither. Mama I don't mean you no disrespect but this is mighty strong." Willie Earl said in an apologetic tone. Mama got up from the table and got me by the hand. 'C'mon baby girl, let's get these clothes pressed and folded. They been calling our names all day", mama said in a voice that was filled with fear and anxiety.

Willie Earl sat down, took a deep breath, and began his story. "Daddy I was in the white barbershop shining shoes and I overheard the men talking about Big Frank. They said that they found his body in the alley behind the Beeline Beauty shop and he had been shot through the head. The white men in the barber shop said they had an idea who may have done it, and they were going to tell the sheriff, and have the person picked up." Willie Earl said in a trembling voice. "Daddy I'm scared. What if they come after you?" Willie Earl moaned. "Calm down boy, ain't nobody coming after me. I haven't done anything to be scared about." Daddy said in a strangled tone I had never heard before.

Daddy turned his back and stared out of the kitchen window. His tall lean frame and strong shoulder muscles seemed to double over and bow down as if the weight of the world were on his shoulders. He finally turned around and said to Willie Earl" get my coat". They were out of the house in a flash.

Mama and I sat in the bedroom on the edge of our chairs and listened intently as we peeked through the crack in the door at my daddy and brother. Mama seemed to wake up from a spell when daddy told Willie Earl to "c'mon." Mama called out of the back door to daddy; "Dial, Dial" but he didn't miss a step. His long legs seemed to connect with the wind as they made tracks down the sidewalk. I had no idea where they were going. Mama and I watched as my brother did his best to keep in step with my daddy.

They finally reached the Johnson house. Mama and I had followed Daddy and Willie Earl at a safe distance; far enough for them not to see us yet close enough to keep them in sight. We ducked behind hedges and trees as we followed them. I fell once and skinned my knee so badly that you could see the white meat. Mama stopped and tied her clean white handkerchief around my badly bleeding knee. I didn't cry. We kept going until we reached the edge of the fence far enough away not to be detected by daddy and Willie Earl but close enough to see what happened.

The sheriff was dragging Mr. Johnson out of his house in handcuffs. Mrs. Johnson was screaming and Lola and her older sisters were pulling Mr. Johnson back into the house. It looked as if they would pull him half into. The sheriff was using his billy club to hit Lola and her sisters to try to get them off of Mr. Johnson but they just screamed louder and pulled even harder. Lola's brothers were helping out at a local farm pulling cane so they were not there to help Mrs. Johnson fight the angry men off of their daddy.

My daddy tried to talk to the sheriff. He was asking the sheriff what Mr. Johnson had done but the sheriff cursed and swore at my daddy to get out of the way. Three deputies came from what seemed liked nowhere and grabbed daddy from behind. They called Daddy a "black son of a bitch". Daddy tried to fight them off. Willie Earl tried to jump in and help but when he jumped in to help the billy club came down hard on the back of his head.

Mama fainted and I yelled "Willie Earl, Willie Earl!" My eyes met my daddy's as the men dragged him into the paddy wagon. Willie Earl lay still on the ground. My daddy shouted "get him home. Get him home, Pookie." "Take care of your mama, I'll see ya'll soon." Daddy yelled through the back door of the wagon.

Tears streamed down my face as I tried to help mama up from the ground. Mama got up and saw Willie Earl lying on the ground. Seems like we got strength from God above and somehow we got my brother home. It was February 16th 2 days before Willie Earl's birthday. He would have been 14 years old. Mama was bent over with what seemed like the weight of the world on her shoulders trying to finish washing the clothes. I was trying to button my dress with my left hand. My fingers still ached from trying to help mama get my brother home from the Johnson's front yard. The doctor had come but he said the blow to Willie Earl's head was so severe that if he survived he would never be the same.

Willie Earl died that night in Mama's arms. She had sat up all night holding his stiff body and rocking him back and forth on the bed. The colored men who worked for Mr.Rooker's funeral home had come to get my brother. They spoke quietly to my mama in the living room. They told her that they would bring the chairs and signs around 2 o'clock the next day.

Mama and I sat holding each other all night long. Sometimes mama would cry out loud. I just closed my eyes and pretended that it was a dream and in the morning everything would be all right. I did dream that night. I dreamed that me, Willie Earl, Sammy, mama, and daddy were sitting on the porch eating ice cream, and laughing and talking. I woke up to find that it was a dream and all the horrible things that had happened the day before were really true.

I went on the back porch and looked at my daddy's shaving mug. The mug had a man with a mustache on the front. Daddy had promised to give that cup to Willie Earl when he got old enough to shave. I picked it up and looked at it real hard for the first time in my life. I held it close to my face. I could smell my daddy's Aqua Velvet after-shave on it. I sat down and started to cry. I felt a hand on my shoulder and I swung around frightened by the touch. It was Lola. Lola's eyes met mine. We fell into each other's arms and we held onto each other for dear life. Lola, Lola, my Lola had come back to me. Lola smiled and the hole where her beautiful white tooth used to be was the most beautiful thing that I had ever seen.

Mama came onto the back porch and told me to come in and help with the dinner. Sammy, Maurva Jean, and Bailey would be home on the evening train, and she wanted everything to be ready when they got there. Mama never said a word to Lola. Even though Lola spoke politely as she always did mama acted as if she didn't see Lola. Mama just turned around and went in the house as if she didn't hear or see Lola. I said bye to Lola and went into the house behind mama before the screened door closed.

Maurva Jean, Bailey, and Sammy all came in on the same train. It was six o'clock when they got to the house on Merritt Street. They had walked all the way from the train depot. The taxicabs for black folks were not allowed to run after 5 pm during the week because of the curfew since Big Frank and Willie Earl's murders.

No one said a word about my brother's murder. I heard mama tell Miss Hattie that she had to sign some papers at the courthouse. The papers said that Willie Earl interfered with the sheriff trying to do his duty and was accidentally hit in the head with the sheriff's nightstick.

It was a gloomy, misty, foggy Saturday morning. I had helped mama get dressed. It was so hard because she could hardly stand up. Her face was swollen and her eyes were puffy. It looked as if someone had stuffed cotton into her cheeks and underneath her eyes.

Everybody had been so nice. The Ladies Aide Society from church had been at our house all week long. The house was full of food sent by neighbors and the people from church. Rev. Tremble and his wife had come every night and sat and talked with mama, Sammy, Maurva Jean and Bailey. I had stayed in my room and hoped and prayed that Willie Earl would wake up and yell at me for hiding under the bed. I remember Rev. Tremble had said in his preaching that you could ask God for whatever you wanted and he would give it to you or make a way for you to get it. I had been praying all week but God hadn't woken up my brother and I was sad.

Lola came to the house everyday and every day we would hide under the bed, and be real still and quiet waiting for the grown folks to leave. One night Maurva Jean had caught us under the bed with a flashlight trying to read the paper that the funeral home men had brought. We were just getting to the part about Willie Earl going home to be with the Lord when she caught us and threatened to tell mama on us. She made Lola go home.

I remember when Lola and I use to hide under the bed and didn't need a flashlight because of Lola's white teeth. Well Lola only had one front tooth now and it had turned black and looked like it might fall out if she breathed too hard.

Bailey stood and stared out at the misty rain. It was gray and ugly and the wind whipped at the shutters as if it wanted to rip them from the house. We all got our coats and hats on. Sammy went outside to fasten the shutters down. He didn't come back in. I didn't have time to think much about it because we were leaving for the church. We walked to church because we did not have enough money for another funeral car. Mama said we barely had enough for the body car. The men from the funeral home told mama that Mr. Rooker had cut the price of the body car as a favor to her for doing his shirts just the way he liked them. We got to the front door and the church was packed with people. Mama and Bailey were in front.

Bailey had locked his arm around mama to keep her from falling. Maurva Jean started screaming and crying. The music from the new organ we had raised money for last summer at the Cake Walk and Chitterling Festival swelled with chords from "Jesus Keep Me Near the cross". Miss Viola's soprano voice could be heard above the moans and groans of the people as we walked into the church." In the cross in the cross be my glory ever". She sang the verse over and over as we walked for what seemed like ten miles before Mama and Bailey got to the front pew. As we walked down the aisle people reached out to mama and grabbed her hand. People patted my head and tapped Bailey on the shoulders. Maurva Jean had fainted and the Ladies Nurse's Guild had taken her to the fainting room. I walked behind mama.

Suddenly, mama and Bailey stopped. I didn't know why they had stopped but all of a sudden Mama yelled out "Willie Earl, Willie Earl, my baby, my baby." I could see her bending over but I didn't know why. Finally Bailey pulled mama back and sat her on the front pew. When they sat down I was able to see what was wrong. I froze in my tracks. The funeral home men looked at me and beckoned for me to come forward. I stood there until I could lift my feet. They felt like someone had tied bricks on them. I stumbled forward and was staring right into the face of my brother. He looked like my brother but in a stiff frozen way. His face had white powder on it like some the ladies wore to church on Sunday. His good suit looked like it was too tight and as if someone had pressed it without first putting a wet cloth on it, like mama had taught us to do in order to keep the shine down. I felt someone pulling me back. It was one of the ladies from the Ladies Nurses Guild. She sat me down and put a cool rag on my head. It felt good.

I watched the funeral home men turn a crank on the box my brother laid in and the choir sang "Oh I Want to See Him". Someone shouted from the back, "wait a minute here come Mr. Dial." I looked back and saw my daddy standing tall and proud handcuffed to the man that had dragged him into the paddy wagon that day at Mr. Johnson's house. The other three deputies walked behind my daddy as he came down the center aisle of the Live Oak Baptist church.

Daddy's face looked different. There were bruises and scratches all over his face and a bandage around his hand. He bent over and kissed mama and he patted my face. His hand brushed across Bailey's back. When he got to the casket where Willie Earl lay so still and straight Daddy bent down on his knees and sobbed. The deputies lifted him up and practically dragged him from the church. As the pastor came to the front to speak a silence fell over the church, and at that moment a small whimper could be heard from the back. I turned my head to see who it was, and just as I remembered what my mama had said about looking back in church, I saw that it was Miss Francine on the back row whimpering and crying over my brother Willie Earl.

When we came inside from the backyard of the church where they had put my brother in a hole in the ground, and thrown the red dirt on top of him until we couldn't see the box anymore we all went to the church Fellowship Hall to eat. All I could see was food piled high on every table. The pastor blessed the food and everyone sat down to eat. Bailey got up and spoke. He told all of the people how grateful he was, but that mama needed to get home to get some rest.

As we left the church people hugged mama and spoke blessings over her. I saw the Johnson family, Miss Viola, Pearline, Coach Solomon and Miss Sutton. I wondered why Coach Solomon was holding Miss Sutton's hand and their shoulders seemed to rub together as they stood looking at us. Miss Sutton blew me a kiss. I smiled at her and looked away before she could see the tears rolling down my cheeks. Miss Francine and Mayor Rooker were standing on the other side of the churchyard. Miss Francine waved her handkerchief at mama, and mama nodded her head at Miss Francine.

We walked into the house. It was warm and had the sweet smell of potato pie in the air. My brother Sammy was sitting on the couch when we got there. Mama told me to get changed and lay down. Maurva Jean had already changed and was lying down. She didn't make it through the service. The ladies had brought her home after she came to herself after fainting at the church. I lay on my bed and listened to the others talk. Sammy explained to mama that the deputies had cut a deal with him. The only way that they would let our daddy come to the services for Willie Earl was if Sammy stayed in jail in his place. They had finger printed Sammy and booked him like he was a criminal. Needless to say word got back to Sammy's college.

Chapter 4

THE COURTHOUSE WAS hot and musty. It was packed with everybody from Madison County. I was sitting in the balcony with mama, Sammy, Miss Viola, Pearline, the Johnson family, some of the men from the barber shop, Miss Sutton, and Coach Solomon. Maurva Jean and Bailey had to get back home. Bailey had to help with the farm and Maurva Jean had to get back to her job at the bookkeeping office.

It seemed so high up in that balcony. I got dizzy trying to look over and see the people downstairs. Lola came and squeezed in between Sammy and me. Mama gazed at Lola and looked away with a funny expression on her face. Lola squeezed my hand and smiled that toothless smile that she had gotten at the hands of Big Frank. Big Frank was the reason we were all here on this hot Saturday morning in July.

The trial had been deliberately set for the weekend because folks in Madison County wouldn't take off their regular jobs for a trial for a "black man" Besides folks around town had said that it wouldn't' take longer than a day to find the man guilty who had killed Big Frank.

Sammy had almost taken the place of Willie Earl as far as bringing us news from around town. He had gotten a letter from the college and read it out loud to mama and me one Sunday afternoon while we sat on the front porch. It said he could come back to school on a "probationary status." Sammy had written them back and told them he couldn't come back right now because his family needed him. Sammy and mama and I cried about that letter all week long.

I saw some men walk in and sit together in a special place. Sammy whispered to Mama that those men were the jurors. They were supposed to be Daddy's peers according to Sammy.

None of those men looked like my daddy. I saw a lot of folks from town sitting in different places in the courtroom. Mr.Rooker, Miss Francine, and Miss Hattie were sitting together. Miss Hattie was sitting next to Miss Francine in her nice blue starched maid's uniform fanning Miss Francine in case she got the vapors and fainted.

Miss Hattie had passed by our house one afternoon on her way home and told mama about how Miss Francine would get to hollering and screaming at Mr. Rooker if he didn't do what she wanted him to do. She told us that one time Miss Francine took the scissors and cut up two of Mr.Rooker's suits and threw them out of the backdoor and told Mr. Rooker where he could go and how fast he could get there. It was pitiful because Mr. Rooker only had three suits to his name according to Miss Hattie. Mama and Miss Hattie laughed and laughed and mama told me to go to bed.

The ladies from the Beeline Beauty Parlor, Mr. Neuman from the grocery store where I went to get thread and turpentine for mama were sitting in a section down front. A man with a deep voice came from a door off to the side of the room and said in a loud voice that made Lola and me almost jump out of our skins, "All rise!" Another man came in wearing what looked to me like a long black choir robe. He immediately picked up a stick and hit it on the big tall desk when he sat down. The desk reminded me of the podium where Pastor stood on Sunday mornings to preach. "Hear ye hear ye the citizen of Atlanta, Georgia, county seat of Madison Criminal Court #164 is now in session, the honorable Haley J. Witherspoon presiding," the deep voiced man said.

The man in the black robe hit the tall desk and the man screaming continued on saying, "please be seated." I looked hard at the man talking and realized who he was. It was the Postman. He looked different without his hat. His shirt was pressed and he was wearing a tie and pants with a heavy belt and what looked like pistol. "But why would anyone have a pistol in a courtroom?" I asked myself loud enough for Lola to hear and answer, "I don't know," and for Sammy to say "hush."

Three deputies came through the door dragging a big man. He couldn't stand on his own because he had metal rings around his ankles, and what seemed like a metal pole between his legs. I think that is why they were dragging him.

His head was bald as if someone had deliberately cut off his hair. He was wearing a uniform of some sort with numbers across the back. His head was down and his shoulders were bent as if he were carrying an invisible sack of potatoes. Behind him came two more deputies dragging a man with the same kind of clothes. This man stood up as straight as he could and looked at everyone in the courthouse like a mad dog. He was my daddy. My daddy was always happy and always hugging and kissing us.

My daddy's face was always clean and shiny. The man down on the floor under me had a face with stubby gray hair, empty eyes and clothes that did not fit his body. No matter how sad he looked he managed to lift his head and connect with us and immediately the bond floated back between daddy and the family.

Mamma sobbed into her handkerchief. Sammy sat up straight in his chair as if to tell daddy that he was taking care of everybody. I stared at my daddy and tried to said "Daddy, daddy", but no words came out. They just stuck in my throat and only a small gurgling sound came out.

The deputies continued to drag the men into the room like hogs that know they are being brought to slaughter. The people in the courtroom fanned with the paper fans from Rooker's funeral home. The people in the colored section fanned with homemade fans, and fans that had been broken by the white folks and thrown in the trash. The black folks got them out of the trashcans, taped them up, and made them like new. Miss Francine had a fan with three white children with folded hands looking up to heaven on the front.

Mr. Rooker had printed the fans and given them out to the white churches as advertisement for his funeral home. As the folks fanned they could see the words on the fans moving back and forth in front of their eyes, "Rooker's funeral home where your loved ones rest in peace." Willie Earl said that one time he was collecting bottles and went into the funeral home basement and saw an awful site. Black folks bodies piled naked on top of each other. The stench was awful. These were bodies of people who could not pay their funeral home bills.

Willie Earl had told us once that there was a big machine in the back of the funeral home where they burned up the people that couldn't pay. I am so glad that mama said we had a fifteen-cent a month policy on everybody in our family because I would not be able to sleep thinking about my brother lying naked in the basement of a funeral home waiting to be burned up.

The tears stung my eyes thinking about my brother. He was my brother and I loved him and I missed him so much. Mama turned all of the mirrors over and put all of Willie Earl's pictures in a box under the bed and hung a black drape over the mirror in the room that he and Sammy had shared. I could feel him next to me sometimes when I sat on the front porch by myself. Willie Earl was gone. "Gone home to be with the Lord," said Pastor Tremble in his home going preaching for my brother's funeral.

All the folks that had come to the house during the week Willie Earl died told my mama how good and natural my brother looked. I didn't know what that meant but I think it was good because mama always smiled when they said it.

Sammy explained to mama that the man sitting in the chair next to where Mr. Johnson and daddy sat was called a public defender. He was going to tell them to let my daddy go free. When the man stood up to talk his blue seersucker suit was soaked through. He kept wiping his forehead with his handkerchief and paced around the room like a banter rooster running from the chopping block. The man in the black robe with the stick asked the man to speak. The man said in a shaky voice; "These boys will plead not guilty your honor". As soon as the words left his mouth the people started screaming, and throwing handkerchiefs and fans everywhere. Some people stood up and called the man a "Nigger lover."

The whole building seemed like it was swaying and would topple over at any minute. Finally, the man in the black robe got everybody to settle down by beating the stick on the tall desk, and promising to throw everybody out if they didn't keep quiet. The man in the blue seersucker suit went on about how my daddy and Mr. Johnson were good colored boys who had never been in any trouble to speak of. He talked about how my daddy had moved here when he got out of the service and was a hard worker who took care of his family

I watched the man and I saw that he was different from the white men I saw from a distance around town. He looked more like the men who had come to give Sammy his scholarship that night on the front porch. His suit looked like one that mama had pressed for Mr. Rooker one time and she had carried on about how that seersucker felt. I touched it and rubbed it but I didn't know what it felt like. I know that it felt different from daddy's Sunday suit that the doctor had given him for working for him one month last year.

I could tell that the blue seersucker suit was different from the pants and jacket that Rev Tremble had given Sammy as a Christmas present one year. When the pants got too short for Sammy they were passed on to Willie Earl, and he wore them to church every Sunday with the coat Sammy had gotten from a rich white family he had worked for serving one of their parties. Those were the same clothes that Willie Earl had worn to go home to be with the Lord. I hope that the Lord will let Willie Earl go right on collecting his bottles because that was his favorite thing to do. I guess he probably would because mama always said that the Lord was a good God. Well if the Lord is so good then why was my daddy sitting downstairs with chains on his hands and feet and Willie Earl dead, and Lola's front tooth missing I hadn't figured out yet.

I looked out of the upstairs courthouse window as the man from the other side of the room went on about how Franklin Roosevelt Simmons had been shot down in cold blood over a two-bit prostitute who had not done one good thing for the community. I saw the smoke rise up to the courthouse window outside and thought that someone must be burning trash and leaves. I heard a boom like the bottle rockets Willie Earl shot for the 4th day of July only ten times louder. I looked around and saw smoke coming into the courthouse. The courtroom started to fill with smoke. A man ran into the courtroom and yelled that "Rooker's funeral home was on fire."

Everybody downstairs ran and tried to get through the courthouse door at the same time. I saw Miss Hattie drag Miss Francine through the side door that all the colored folks had come through that morning before we all climbed the old rickety stairs that led to the balcony where we sat staring at the commotion below.

After all the white folks got out we all filed down the stairs and went out of the same door we came in that morning. The afternoon sun hurt my eyes and I used my hands to shade them. Mama had packed fried chicken and cold potato salad for us for lunch. We sat down on the rocks on the shady side of the courthouse. Lola found us and sat down to eat with us. Sammy went off to help with the fire and to find out what made the funeral home catch on fire. We washed ourselves in the outside pump and watched as Mr. Rooker's funeral home burned to the ground. Sammy came around the corner and told us one of the most awful stories I can remember. It seems that one of the men that took care of the dead bodies in the funeral home had gotten drunk and poured too much fluid in the tube. The other man that was with him realized what had happened and barely escaped with his life. He told Rooker that the old man was smoking a cigarette and he and the body had caught fire and the whole place blew up. Sammy said that bodies were thrown all over the street and people were crying and screaming. Some folks were looking for their kinfolk that had been waiting to be funeralized at Rookers. Worst of all some of the bodies were naked and some were burned so badly that you couldn't tell black from white. Some folks were threatening to sue Mr. Rooker. The paddy wagon had to take Mr. Rooker to the jailhouse and lock him up to keep him from being killed by the white folks.

The bell on top of the courthouse rang so loudly that I jumped off of the rock where I was sitting. We went back to the courthouse and the man with the loud voice came to the door and told everybody to go home and come back when they called us to come back.

It was getting late in the afternoon. We all waited to hear the call to go back to the courthouse. Sammy went out to check the mail. He came back inside with a letter in his hands and his eyes filled with tears. He told mama it was a letter from Uncle Sam. I looked at mama and said I didn't know we had an Uncle Sam. This Uncle Sam wanted my brother Sammy to come to a place called Fort Mac. He wanted Sammy to come soon. I didn't understand. But I knew this was not a good thing by the way mama cried and Sammy sat on the couch with his head in his hands. Uncle Sam told my brother in the letter to only bring a bag with a change of clothes and a toothbrush. He would give him everything else. I started to think that maybe our Uncle

Sam wasn't so bad after all until mama told me that Uncle Sam wanted my big brother to fight in a war. My brother never even got in a fight in school how he could fight a war.

Mama, Pearline, Sammy, Maurva Jean, Bailey, Maurva Jean's husband T-Bo, and I rode to the train station in T-Bo and Maurva Jean's car. It was amazing. We all got into that car and had room to stretch our legs. Even Maurva Jean had room. Her stomach had gotten so fat that I thought she would pop. Mama said Maurva Jean was in a family way. I didn't know what that meant until a month later.

We all waited in the car for the train. The windows got all fogged up from all of the talking and laughing going on in that car. Sammy was leaving and we were all trying to be brave and pretend that it was all right. Mama and Sammy had talked all night about a place called Europe. I tried to find it on the big map at school. Miss Sutton had helped me find it and she gave me a funny look, patted me on my head and walked away. The train came way too soon and it was hard not to cry. Sammy was going away. I loved Sammy and told him I would send him my pictures and drawings every day. Sammy always made me put my school drawings and poems on the icebox. He said I had talent. He always said I had a lot going on in my little "big head." I already had lots of pictures and little stories in my treasure box to send to Sammy while he was away. Hopefully it wouldn't be too long.

The next morning Maurva Jean and T-Bo left in their big car. They let Bailey drive because T-Bo said it was good for him to drive a real car instead of a tractor all the time.

Bailey really liked driving because he was grinning so wide that you could see the back of his head through the gap in his front teeth. Mama was always telling Bailey to close his mouth before a fly went down his throat.

Maurva Jean wobbled to the car and T-Bo helped her into the back seat so that she could stretch out and her feet wouldn't swell. T-Bo hopped in front next to Bailey. They waved to us and the car went quickly down the road. When mama and I got back to the house on Merritt Street we sat on the porch and thought of happier times.

Mama was in the kitchen frying sausages for our dinner when Mr. Curtis from the barbershop knocked on the front door. Mr. Curtis always had a fancy haircut with a part on the side. He had a small moustache that had points on the ends. His lips were thin and his mouth was small. He always talked fast and flung his hands around when he talked. Mama invited him in the house and gave him a glass of iced tea. Mr. Curtis told mama "this iced tea is so good Miss Bea, you know iced tea is the house wine of the south." He said in his squeaky high-pitched voice. Mama smiled and asked him what brought him out this way. Well Miss Bea, the trial is going to start back up tomorrow and things don't look so good. They want you and my wife to testify. "Miss Bea, do you remember if your husband brought in a sack that night when he came back from the barber shop? Curtis asked?" Mama sat up in her chair with a frown on her face trying to remember. I remembered right away. Then mama spoke up. I do remember seeing a sack. I remember Dial telling

Sammy to do something with it but I don't know what he did with it.

I was standing in the doorway when mama called me to the kitchen. Annie baby have you seen a sack lying around anywhere in the house or the yard, she asked? Willie Earl had made me swear on the bible that I wouldn't tell anybody about that sack.

The courthouse opened early the next morning and mama and me were the first ones in line at the door that the colored folks went through. Mama had our lunch basket on one arm, and her bag, which was filled with everything we would need for the long day ahead on the other arm. Mr. Curtis and mama talked a long time last night and we didn't get to bed until late. Mr. Curtis told mama that she could visit daddy at the jail on Sunday. He told her that she should bring him some underwear, some cigarettes, toothpaste, soap, and a toothbrush.

Mama had stayed up long after Mr. Curtis left getting everything ready and I stayed up with her. Needless to say I was very sleepy when we got to the courthouse. We sat in our seats and they seemed harder than I remembered. It was so hot that everyone in the room looked like somebody had poured oil over their heads.

I looked down and saw everyone in place. Daddy came in with the deputies, surrounding him. Mr. Johnson came in next with deputies surrounding him. They both looked so thin and so tired. Before Sammy left to go to Uncle Sam to fight in the war he explained to mama and me who all of the people in the room were and what they did. The man at the big desk was the judge. The postman was the bailiff, and the people in the special box that always sat together were the jurors. Sammy had told me that he was depending on me to pay close attention and write to him every day to let him know what was going on. I sat up straight and listened closely.

The bailiff yelled out that it was time to get started and the judge banged on the desk. Everyone stood up and sat down quickly. The judge said it was already 90 degrees and he wanted to get this over with before noon so folks could go on their way and get their chores and errands done. The man with the glasses and seersucker suit spoke first. He was daddy's lawyer appointed by the state. Sammy had explained to me that he was a white man from North Atlanta. He stood up and said that all the things that they said my daddy had done was circumstantial and that there were no eyewitnesses. He told the judge that the case should be dismissed.

I had a hard time writing down circumstantial but Lola was sitting right beside me and she was the best speller in Madison County's Colored Elementary School. She had once won a ribbon for her spelling. She took the pencil from my hand and wrote down everything that the judge and the lawyer said. Lola was my best friend.

When the lawyer from North Atlanta spoke the people yelled and threw paper and fans. The judge told them he would throw everybody out if it happened again. The lawyer that wanted my daddy to go to jail stood up and spoke. He said that my daddy had killed Big Frank in cold blood. He said that daddy and Mr. Johnson had beaten Big Frank and shot him in the head. He said that the gun had been found in Mr. Johnson's house with his fingerprints on it. He also said that Mr. Johnson had so many children that he could not feed them, and that Mr. Johnson had put his girls on the street as prostitutes to get money for the family because Mr. Johnson couldn't keep a job.

When he finished the whole upstairs section where we sat was crying and murmuring. The judge told them that he would dismiss all of the upstairs if they made any more sounds. He told the jurors to go and to be back in one hour with their decision. He said one hour and no longer because he had to be over in Fulton by 2 o'clock and as it was he would not be able to have lunch. He banged down the stick on the desk and the jurors left the room.

We all went out in the 12:0'clock sun. Mama had brought along lunch and a big umbrella. We went to the backside of the courthouse and waited for the hour to pass. As we sat and waited we watched the men working to rebuild Rooker's funeral home/mayor's office. They were almost done with the frame. It looked bigger than the old funeral home. Some of the men waiting with us outside of the courthouse talked to mama and the other folks waiting. They said that old man Rooker had lied to the insurance company and told them that a gas leak from one of the machines had caused the fire. They had given Rooker over six thousand dollars. They said that his wife, Miss Francine had men working at their house night and day, knocking out walls and building rooms. She was going to have her dream house at last.

Everybody in town was talking about Mr. Rooker's hair falling out in chunks by the day. He had to make the part lower on the side of his head. They all laughed so hard that Mr. Curtis from the barbershop fell on the ground slobbering. His laughing was catching because the whole group on the backside of the courthouse was laughing so hard that we didn't hear the first call to come back into the courthouse.

Lola's little brother had to come and get us. We all went back to our seats. I could see mama's lips moving and hear the whispered prayers coming from her lips. The judge asked the jurors if they could tell him if the men were guilty or innocent. The judge asked my daddy and Mr. Johnson to please stand and face the jury. The man on the front row of the jury stood and told the judge that Mr. Johnson was guilty of murder in the first degree. They also said that daddy was not guilty of murder but guilty of accompanying him.

The courtroom went wild. People were screaming nigger, coon, and darkie. One man stood and said if that nigger goes free I'll kill him myself. The people screamed and yelled until I thought my eardrums would burst. Before I could shed a tear I saw Lola running down the stairs from the colored section where we were sitting. Her mother yelled softly, "Lola get back here." Lola didn't turn back. She did not stop until she was standing right in front of the man with the black choir robe. Lola screamed out; "Let my daddy go, he didn't hurt nobody. Big Frank hurt me bad. He tore off my clothes, he hurt my privates, and he pushed his privates in my privates and then put his privates in my mouth. He put his privates in my behind. Then he relieved himself on me. He hurt me. He hurt me bad. He made blood come out of me." Lola fell to the floor sobbing.

By that time Lola's mama had gotten to her. You could hear a pin fall on cotton in that hot musty courtroom that dark, dark day in July. Lola's daddy had tried to get up to help his daughter but the deputies had held him back. Lola's mama and some of the other ladies took her outside. The judge sat still and his eyes seem to roll back and forth in his head like the hands on a clock that has been wound too tight. The jurors whispered to each other.

The white folks in the courtroom all had worried looks on their faces and they twisted and squirmed in their seats. They finally found their voices. Miss. Francine stood up and yelled; "Let them go! Do you hear me? Let them go I say!" Miss Hattie and old man Rooker were trying to get her to sit down and be quiet but she wouldn't. Miss Hattie tried fanning her. Mr.Rooker tried cooing at her and calling her baby. Nothing worked. Miss Francine was going to have her say. "If you don't let them go I'll call everyone of you out. You know I can do it. "Shall I start with you Billy? I can tell your wife where you were last Friday night, and the rest of you so called jurors."

The white folks were yelling and calling Miss Francine a nigger lover and crazy. The judge banged and banged on the desk until the courtroom went silent. Miss Francine finally sat down and Miss Hattie fanned her robustly as if her own life depended on it. Mr. Rooker took out one of his handkerchiefs and wiped his head and face until his bald spot shined like a new penny. His suit was completely soaked through. You could see the outline of his under shirt right through his suit.

When the judge got everybody quiet he told the jurors to go and not come back until they could figure everything out. He said he had to get over to Fulton for a trial involving a white man and a colored woman getting married. Before he hit the stick down he looked around the courtroom, then up in the balcony where we all sat and he said" I don't know what this world is coming to with white folks letting nigras run wild and marry outside their race. Get out and don't come back until you all are called, dismiss."

Chapter 5

HALEY J. WITHERSPOON was a man that people did not want to mess around with. Judge Witherspoon was called the "hanging judge" according to Miss Hattie. Miss Hattie had stopped by our house the evening after that awful day in court when Miss Francine had told the judge to let my daddy and Mr. Johnson go. She told mama that old Judge Witherspoon always stopped at the Rooker's home when he was in town. Word had it that he loved Miss Hattie's cooking. Miss Hattie and mama laughed out loud because they both knew how much they contributed to the white community; not by choice but out of necessity. Mama kept all of the rich white folks clothes cleaned, and nobody was a better cook than Miss Hattie. Hattie was the only woman the white folks would let cook for their parties.

Miss Hattie told mama that Judge Witherspoon had spent the night at the Rookers' when Mr. Rooker was at his funeral directors meetings. She told mama that Miss

Francine was a different woman when old judge was around. Yes, Hattie grinned as she spoke "Miss Francine laughed and danced all around the judge, and dressed up in her black nightgown and bed jacket. She looked like a fly in the buttermilk." said Miss Hattie. Then Miss Hattie laughed so hard her top teeth fell out of her mouth onto the floor. I rushed over and picked them up and handed them to mama. Miss Hattie snatched them out of mama's hands, wrapped them in her handkerchief, and stormed out. She let the screen door slam behind her. I asked mama, Why did Miss Hattie's teeth fall out? Mama said "Lord child you don't want to know, you don't want to know."

Mr. Curtis came to the house on Monday July12th. I was on the porch in the hammock. He walked up and spoke to me and then asked for mama. Mama came out wiping her hands on her apron and invited him in. Mr. Curtis looked different. His clothes were wrinkled and his hair was not brushed. He and mama walked into the kitchen and talked in low tones. Then all of a sudden I heard mama yell out "Oh my God."

I jumped from the hammock and ran into the kitchen. "Miss Bea I have searched high and low for that sack but I can't find it." Curtis said in his high squeaky voice. "Your husband said it has got to be here at the house". Daddy didn't know what Willie Earl had done with the sack. I stood there with my mouth opened and my eyes bulging out of my head. Beads of sweat popped across my forehead. Mama looked at me and asked, "What's the matter baby you feeling sick?" I stood there and wished that I were Willie

Earl. Willie Earl was such a cool liar. He could make up a lie and not bat an eye. Me, I couldn't lie on a rug straight, let alone tell mama a lie. Mama had a way of making you tell the truth by just looking at you. "Annie, Annie." mama called. I finally found my tongue, which felt as thick as molasses. I was able to squeak out a "yes ma'am." "Baby you go lay down and I'll bring you a cool rag for your head." Mama said in her soothing voice. I turned and flew back to the hammock.

I laid there trying to figure out what to do. I wish that Sammy or Willie Earl were here, they would know what to do. I dozed off into a fitful sleep. I woke up and Lola was standing over me with her big fat braids hanging from her wooly head. "Why you outside sleeping in this broke down hammock?" asked Lola, as see leaned over me and pressed her hands into my chest. "Cause I want to." I said. "Anyway get off me, before you break the hammock down with your big ole feet." I squealed. "I ain't got no big feet". Lola said. "But I do got this." Lola opened her mouth and showed me the funniest thing I had ever seen. Lola had taken a piece of tin foil and wrapped it around the one front tooth she had left. I laughed so hard that I rolled out of the hammock and hit the porch floor with a thud.

"What you laughing at with your nappy head?" asked Lola indignantly. I just kept right on laughing. My tickle box had turned upside down. I laughed so hard I started to cough. Lola grabbed me up by my arm. "I said stop that laughing" Lola said with her jaws all puffed out. "I 'm gonna tell you one mo time, then I'm gonna give you two black eyes and button your nose." Lola said with her fist stuck in my face. "Okay, Okay," I said as I tried not to laugh anymore. We sat there looking into each other's eyes daring each other not to laugh. After about five seconds of both of us trying not to laugh, we burst out into a laughing fit.

We rolled around on the porch until mama called from the house, "Annie, you come in here right now, and Lola you go home!" I waved bye to Lola, and opened the screened door, as I said, "yes mama" I brushed off my clothes, and ran through the screen door before it could slam shut. I looked back just in time to see Lola round the bushes at the end of the yard. Lola was my best friend.

When I saw mama and Mr. Curtis sitting at the table I came back to myself. I had promised Willie Earl on the bible that I would never tell anyone about the sack. Lola and me had buried that sack at the end of the field. We had dug a hole so deep that it took us two days to finish it.

We never did open the sack to see what was in it. We just buried it because my dead brother had made me promise on the bible never to tell anyone about it. He was my brother and the bad men had killed him with their big sticks. They had hit my brother in the head while mama and I watched. I stood there and the tears rolled down my cheeks and into my mouth for my brother Willie Earl. "He was gone home to be with the Lord," Pastor Tremble said in his preaching at my brother's funeral. "Faith." said Pastor Tremble "would see us through." I wish faith would hurry up and see me through because I was going blind with grief for my brother who was dead.

As Mr. Curtis finished his tea he stood up, and told my mama that the sack was the only thing that stood between my daddy, Mr. Johnson and the electric chair." If they didn't get the sack fast, there were enough white folks in this town that believed just like old Judge Witherspoon, that the only "good nigra " was a "dead nigra." Mr. Curtis said as he shook his head sadly.

As I watched, Mr. Curtis walked down the steps and disappeared around the bushes at the edge of the street. I didn't know what to think. I stood in the middle of the kitchen and watched mama begin to tear the house on Merritt Street apart looking for the sack.

It was seven o'clock Friday morning and mama and I were walking back from taking Miss Francine her laundry. Mr. Neuman was waving at us from across the street. He was waving like he wanted us to come to the store. We waved back and crossed the street to see what was wrong. Mr. Neuman waved for us to come inside. He pointed to the telephone and said in his funny voice." Phone call for you, long distance", he said. Mr. Neuman was the only person we knew close by that had a phone and would let us use it. We never used it except one time when my daddy had to talk to his brother up in Detroit to tell him that their daddy had died.

Mama and daddy had gotten enough donations to get daddy's brother a bus ticket to come to Alabama for the funeral. Daddy had walked and hitched rides to get to Alabama for his daddy's funeral. Mama picked up the phone like it was a snake or something that would bite her. Mama almost yelled into the phone. "Hello." said mama shakily. The voice on the other end said that Maurva Jean had a baby girl and everybody was fine. I knew what they said because mama had repeated every word. Mama thanked Mr. Neuman and told him. "Mr. Neuman "bring me a load of laundry and I will do it for free." We walked to the house holding hands and smiling at the good news about Maurva and the baby.

At last some good news had come to Merritt Street.

It was early in the morning and I heard voices in the kitchen. Miss Hattie, Mama, and Miss Viola were busy making tuna, biscuits, sausages, and a lot of other things that looked like what Sammy used to bring home from the white folks parties to our house.

Miss Sutton and Coach Solomon were getting married at the Live Oak Baptist church that morning. Miss Sutton had asked me to carry some flowers and wear a dress she had ordered for me from the Sears Roebuck catalog. We were working hard to get the food to the church as well as my new clothes and ourselves.

Mama had fussed over my hair and pressed it until it hung down my back like the ribbons on a Christmas present. Mama had greased me with so much homemade lard that I was scared that the flies would carry me away. I had shined my shoes with a biscuit left over from breakfast that morning. Mama had wrapped my shoes in a dishrag and put them in the box with all of the other things we would need at the church. When we got to the church all the ladies were busy decorating the church and the fellowship hall. I had never seen the church and fellowship hall look so pretty. Mama had spent the whole week asking folks to bring their best flowers from their yards to the church Saturday morning, and they did. I had never seen so many flowers in one place.

Mr. Neuman had sent over a box of ribbon that he had a hard time selling. They were pink, and had little embroidered flowers on them. Mr. Rooker had even sent a big thing from the funeral home that had candles stuck all around it. It was silver and had little knobs on it. Miss Hattie told us that it was one that Miss Francine kept at her house for her fancy parties.

Mama was helping me to get dressed. She tied a head rag around my hair so that it would stay straight on my head. Mama had on her navy blue church dress with the white lace collar that you pinned on and took off when you got ready to wash the dress. Miss Francine had given mama that dress one Christmas because Mama had gone everyday to Miss Francine's house to help with her mama when she was sick

Willie Earl said that Miss Francine's mama was crazy in the head. She sat on the back porch and talked to her husband who had been dead a long time. Willie Earl told me that one time he was in the shed putting laundry in the Croaker sack, and Miss Eugenie came right in their and pulled her dress up and peed on the laundry that he was putting in the Croaker sack. Needless to say Willie Earl told me that he ran home so fast that lighting couldn't strike him.

I heard mama tell my daddy one night that Miss Eugenie's husband had run off with the waitress at the drugstore and since that time Miss Eugenie hadn't been in her right mind. I went with Willie Earl one time to get the Rooker's laundry and I saw Miss Eugenie sitting on the porch rocking back and forth. She looked like she was sleeping with her eyes opened. She had brown snuff all over the front of her dress and little streams of juice were running from the corners of her mouth and onto the navy blue dress with the white collar that she was wearing. It looked just like the one mama was wearing now, but that couldn't be because mama's dress was clean and smooth. Mama had pressed it just this morning using a damp cloth so it wouldn't shine, and it didn't have a stain on it. Mama looked beautiful.

We finally got my dress over my head. The dress had come with a big pink bow. Mama and Miss Hattie had fussed over that bow for at least five minutes, but after they finished, it looked beautiful. Mama told me to look in the picture mirror in the hall. I did and I didn't know who that girl was in the mirror. That girl had long ringlets of hair, a shiny face and a beautiful dress. Miss Ornie, one of the ladies from the Ladies Aide Society said that I looked like a doll. I couldn't believe it.

I went back and took a peek. I jumped in front of the mirror. I walked past real fast and looked back. I did every trick I could but it was still me. That girl in the hall picture mirror was me, Annie "Pookie" Harris. Just then I heard music. I heard the sounds coming from the new church organ. It wasn't a song that I had heard before. This music was different. It didn't even sound like songs I had heard Sammy play on his radio when he was home. Mama tapped me on my shoulder; and said, "Hey there pretty little girl, it's time for you to go in now."

I had come to the church yesterday with mama to practice walking down the center aisle of the Live Oak Baptist church. I don't know why I had to practice because I walked down the aisle with mama and daddy to get to our same seats every Sunday morning. But I found out pretty quick about how different it was.

There was a lady telling everybody how to walk and how to stand. I remember the lady because she was in my school's office. I saw her there when I had to take the attendance card to the school office for Miss Sutton. She was sitting at the desk with the typewriter. Everybody in the classroom got a turn to take the card. When it was my turn, in the row where I sat in the classroom I felt so excited walking down to the big office and seeing all of the pretty ladies and fancy machines in the office.

Mama whispered to me" Go on now and walk one two like they showed you last night'. Mama opened the door of the Live Oak Baptist church and I froze in my tracks. There were flowers and candles, and the ribbons from Mr. Neuman's store tied in little bows on every bench. There was a long white sheet going down the middle of the church. I know I wasn't supposed to walk on that sheet with my shoes on. I might get mud on it. Mama pushed me and I propelled into the room. She yelled softly, "Throw out the flowers baby" and I did as I walked down the center on the white sheet at Live Oak Baptist church.

There were people in every pew. They were all looking at me and smiling. Miss Viola, Miss Hattie, Pearline, Auntie Chauncey, the whole Johnson family, the Ladies Aide group, some of the teachers from my school, Mrs. Tremble, Mr. Curtis, and his family, people from town that I only knew by face, and the colored men who had come to our house from Rooker's funeral home when Willie Earl died.

I walked until I got down front and stood on the spot that had the little x on it. I closed my eyes real tight and I could see Willie Earl standing in front of me smiling.

When I opened my eyes I saw something so beautiful that it took my breath away! Everybody stood up, I guess to get a better look. There walking right in front of me was what looked like an angel all wrapped in white. When the angel got closer I could tell that it was Miss Sutton. She looked different from the way she looked in the classroom. She had a long piece of white net over her face and her dress was so white and shiny. She had red lips and the same white powder that the other ladies wore on their faces on Sunday. She was walking with a man. I thought I recognized him but I couldn't remember right now. She stopped right in front of Rev. Tremble. All of a sudden Coach Solomon turned around and stood next to Miss Sutton.

I had not looked up at all of the men on the other side of the room until Coach Solomon moved and the man standing with Miss Sutton sat down. I heard Rev. Tremble talking but I couldn't understand a word he was saying.

Then I saw something I had never seen before. Coach Solomon lifted up Miss Sutton's net that was covering her face and he kissed her right on her red mouth. I had only seen Sammy kiss Pearline in the dark on the porch that hot night before he left for school. I had seen daddy kiss mama on the face and me on the forehead. But this was in the broad open daylight, in the church, in front of all of the people. I didn't know what to do or think. I just stood there staring. Finally. One of the ladies took me by the hand and we walked down the aisle of the Live Oak Baptist church while the people clapped and cheered.

Everyone ate cake and drank punch from little cups. Mama and me, Miss Viola, Auntie Chauncey, the Ladies Aide Society, and Miss Hattie had cleaned up everything and were all walking home when a car came whizzing by. It was Miss Sutton and Coach Solomon sitting in the back seat and Mr. Curtis was driving. We waved them out of sight. Mama told Miss Viola, "We be seeing some babies soon". I couldn't wait to tell Lola what they said. Lola had taken Willie Earl's place for explaining things to me and I couldn't wait to tell her this.

We had just gotten home and changed our clothes when Lola came running up to our porch screaming out my mama's name. "Miss Bea! Miss Bea! Miss Bea"! Mama and I came running at the same time. "What in the world is it child?" asked Mama. Lola could hardly catch her breath. "They said all folks that got business with the Johnson / Harris trial is to meet court Monday morning 8 o'clock sharp. Old Judge Witherspoon just announced it". "Mr.

Rooker had done gone over to Donaldsonville for his funeral directors meeting." Lola said breathlessly. I was helping Miss Hattie clean up and wash the dishes after Miss Francine had her Ladies Club in for breakfast and I heard Miss Hattie tell the yardman that it was a good thing that Mr. Rooker had gone to his funeral directors meeting cause that would give Miss Francine time to work old Judge Witherspoon over.

Chapter 6

Miss Hattie had gone to Miss Francine's house earlier that morning to fix breakfast for Miss Francine's ladies group. Miss Hattie had told us that Miss Francine had let her off work for the rest of the morning but she had to work that afternoon and evening.

Miss Hattie slipped quietly into the back door of the Rooker's house. She changed from her regular clothes to her maid's uniform. She started to work cleaning up the dishes. There were wine bottles everywhere. Miss Francine had made such a mess. There were cigarette butts in all of the ashtrays. There were clothes strewn all over the chairs and floor. Miss Hattie picked up the men's pants and right away knew that they were not Mr. Rooker's. They were too small to be Mr. Rooker's and the cloth was real wool polyester.

When she started to fold them a wallet fell out of the pocket and opened on the floor. When Hattie went to pick it up pictures fell out. There were lots of pictures of Miss Francine in various poses. In some of the pictures she was naked as a jaybird. In some of the other pictures she was half naked. Hattie put the pictures back in the wallet, put the wallet back in the pocket, and laid the pants on the settee.

She took her handkerchief out of her apron pocket and wiped her wet face because it was dripping with sweat. Just then old Judge Witherspoon came from the bedroom. He was wearing his boxer drawers and an undershirt. He had a cigar in his mouth but it wasn't lit. He looked at Hattie like he didn't see her, picked up his pants and disappeared back into the bedroom. Hattie went back to the kitchen to finish cleaning up.

About fifteen minutes later the front door creaked open and Hattie looked out of the kitchen window and saw Judge Witherspoon make dust tracks with his car.

Francine Rooker woke up and found herself dressed in her blue nightgown, and tucked under the covers in a way that only Hattie could do. She tried to sit up but her head was pounding like somebody had hit her with a sledgehammer. Francine rolled over and looked at the big cuckoo clock on the wall. It was 4:15. She had exactly 45 minutes to get up and make herself decent before Charlie Rooker would pull the Packard into the carport. She was in no mood to tangle with Charlie Rooker. Her head was pounding from the cheap wine she and old Judge Haley Witherspoon had drunk the night before. Her eyeballs hurt and her face was puffy.

Hattie, she had to find Hattie. Hattie knew exactly what to do for her headache and puffy face. Hattie had fixed her up before and Charlie Rooker never even knew she had gotten sloppy drunk the night before. Francine tried to sit up on the side of the bed but the room swirled around so fast that she almost vomited right on the spot. Every time she tried to call Hattie she had to lay down flat on her back to keep from hurling her insides out on the shiny wooden bedroom floor. Damn that Hattie, where was she when she needed her.

The hot Georgia sun streamed through the curtains and drenched the room in strong yellow rays. The room was neat and orderly. Across the room the chenille bedspread with the light blue balls was draped over the back of the rocking chair. The scent of lemon and verbena permeated the air in the room. These were all signs that Hattie was nearby. Francine tried once more to call for Hattie. Just as she tried to call Hattie's name she heard a car horn outside of the window. She knew without a doubt that it was Charlie Rooker's Chevrolet. Francine tried with all of her might to get up out of the bed but fell back with a pounding headache.

Mr. Rooker came into the house yelling "Cine." Cine was what Charlie called Francine when he was either drunk or happy that he had a funeral parlor full of dead bodies.

Hattie rushed in and gave Mr. Rooker a tall glass of iced tea, cooed all over him, took his hat, and told him to be real quite because Miss Francine had the vapors and she was trying to recover before dinnertime. Rooker believed Hattie's cool lie because Hattie had worked for them since Francine's baby had died or something Hattie had told him. He never even saw the body but he believed Hattie.

Hattie had proven herself trustworthy because he had left liquor and money lying around and it was always in the same place when he went to check it. Hattie was one of the few colored people that he trusted. That colored man that Hattie's friend, Bea was married to made him uneasy. He wanted to see that nigra hanged even though he knew that he (Dial) had not laid one hand on Big Frank. "Big Frank deserved to have his brains blown out for trying to double cross him and his friends from the Big Sun grocery store". When we get that sack we will all rest easier." Rooker said under his breath but loud enough that Hattie heard him. "If I can keep Francine quiet that nigra will hang and it would all be over." Rooker droned on. Hattie pretended not to hear him "Mr. Charlie, Mr. Charlie you heard what I said?" "What?' "Oh yeah Hattie I heard you." "Just give me my supper on the back porch." Rooker said. "Yes sir Mista Charlie. I be getting it right now. " Hattie said quickly.

It's hot as hell in here." Rooker said as he took his tie and suit jacket off and flung them on the new settee that Miss Francine and the postman were sitting on that day that he came home early. Rooker didn't say anything but the scowl on his face clearly showed his disgust. Why he trusted that woman after all the times she had disgraced him he did not know. He had met her in Alabama at the Officer's Club. She was pretty and had the nicest body. She was petite and one of the few women that didn't tower over his five foot four round frame. Francine was always in the club. One night a fight broke out. One of the guys Francine was suppose to be going out with had accused her of being seen walking around with one of the colored boys at the Negro Soldier's Club. Francine had been beaten up pretty bad.

Rooker had felt sorry for her. He took her to the doctor on the base and had her stitched up. He rented a room and let her stay there for a week. Francine said she was grateful and wanted to pay him back one day when her money came in.

Rooker told her not to worry about it. Francine started to hang around wherever Rooker was. He asked her to marry him and move to Georgia. He told her he wanted to start a funeral home business when he got out of the service, and needed a smart pretty woman to run it for him. Francine got drunk one night and told Rooker she would marry him. It was her chance to start over in a new place.

They got married and came to Georgia. They have been together every since. Hattie fixed Mr. Rooker's supper and fixed him some more iced tea with a little of his own bourbon whiskey mixed in with the tea. Mr. Rooker always kept the whiskey way in the back of the kitchen pantry. Hattie mixed it with the tea because she knew that the tea would have old man Rooker out like a light in about 15 minutes. Then she could tend to Miss Francine. She served Mr. Rooker and waited for the tea to take effect.

Hattie walked into the room and saw Miss Francine sprawled across the bed with her nightgown over her head and her feet dangling from the edge of the bed. "Lord I haven't seen her this bad off since she had that baby that came out of her body all brown and fat with curly hair and big brown eyes. I fixed her and the bed good and tight before I left out this afternoon. She must have been trying to get up." Hattie mumbled to herself.

Miss Francine and Hattie had a long history of watching out and covering for each other. Francine had witnessed Hattie kill a woman in the kitchen of her house. Francine threatened to have Hattie sent to jail for killing the woman who was messing round with my husband if she ever mentioned the baby's looks to anybody.

Miss Francine had come into the kitchen just as Hattie had swung the long butcher knife that they used to cut the chickens' heads off after they had rung their necks until they were dead. The woman who stole Hattie's husband had come to Miss Francine's house early that morning while Hattie was fixing breakfast for Miss Francine's ladies group and told Hattie that she and James Lee were leaving on the six o'clock train and she couldn't stop them. Vera Jackson was the lowest trash woman in Madison County and everybody black and white knew it.

Vera Jackson had pushed Hattie too far that time. Hattie grabbed the butcher knife and swung with all of the force in her big frame. Vera's head snapped back and her eyes bulged out like a magpie caught in a trap. Blood sprouted all over the kitchen like someone had turned on a water spicket. Hattie was covered with blood. Her perfectly starched light blue uniform- that she took so much pride in wearing- was soaked in blood, because when Vera fell, she fell backwards and her arms flapped around like a butterfly leaving a flower and landed right into Hattie's arms.

Just as everything happened Miss Francine walked in the back door. She covered her mouth to stifle a scream. Miss Francine and Hattie had worked for two hours cleaning with vinegar and Clorox until the whole house smelled of Clorox. It burned Hattie's eyes and made Miss Francine's skin turn red. They put the body in one of Mr. Rooker's body bags that he kept in the basement for emergency runs. Needless to say the two were jumpier than a toad on a spring lily pad as they entertained Francine's ladies group that morning.

Francine told Hattie how important it was that they went on like nothing had happened and somehow they did even though Hattie had killed a woman and Francine had helped to cover up the crime that cool Monday morning in March.

Hattie called out to Miss Francine as she lifted her up into a sitting position. Miss Francine was the only woman Hattie knew that lost weight after having a baby and even though it was years later Miss Francine had never gotten over having to let the baby go. Mr. Rooker had believed Hattie when she said that the baby was still born and had died in the womb. She had told Rooker that the baby's wind had been cut off and had died in the womb and had turned dark from not having air for such a long time. Hattie told Rooker she would take care of everything and keep things quite so folks wouldn't know and talk about how Francine couldn't hold a baby with her little child like frame. Francine had suffered three miscarriages and this would have been her fourth. Even though Rooker was familiar with death he believed everything Hattie said because he couldn't bear to know the real truth. None of them could stand any more of that. Francine called out to Hattie in a drunken slur. "Hattie, Hattie, where were you when I needed you? Where is Rooker? He didn't see me did he? Oh Hattie. I'm so scared. Help me. Help me." Francine wailed.

Hattie had cleaned Miss Francine up and spread salve on her eyes to take the swelling down and bring the color back to her cheeks. Hattie had made hot sulfur tea and made Francine drink it all down. Francine had complained about the bitter tea and how it made her gag and made her bowels loose. In spite of her complaining Francine trusted Hattie because she had brought her through before. Hattie and Francine had been through hell and back together and both women trusted each other with their lives. Hattie got Francine all cleaned up and back to her natural self by the time Mr. Rooker woke up from his whiskey induced sleep.

Monday morning came fast. It was raining hard and the wind was blowing. It was what daddy called "raining cats and dogs". No matter how hard everybody tried to hold onto their hats and umbrellas the wind blew them away like the Easter eggs Willie Earl and I made from parchment paper and put them in front of the blower on the stove. They would float across the kitchen and land on the table or the floor on the other side of the room.

The courthouse was packed. The white folks packed the inside from top to bottom. So all of the colored folk had to wait outside in the pouring rain. Mama tried to cover me with her coat but the rain just came down harder and the wind blew stronger.

Lola was standing next to me. She had an umbrella that was turned inside out from the wind. She still held onto it as if it was keeping the rain off of her. Mrs. Johnson stood next to her. Tears were streaming down her face. Even though she was soaking wet I still could tell the tears from the rain on her face.

Finally, a white man came to the door and told us we could stand inside the doors, but we couldn't go in because it was already over crowed with people. Mama was close enough to hear what was going on inside. I sat down on the floor and watched the water run off of the people onto the floor of that crowded little space in the front of the courthouse. No one complained. Everyone just stood quietly, listened, and waited. I could hear the people talking but I couldn't understand what they were saying. Mr. Curtis had made his way to where we were standing. He got next to mama and Mrs. Johnson. "I can hear them," Mr. Curtis said in a whisper. Mr. Curtis was telling mama and the rest of us that the judge said that due to the evidence in the case Dial Harris was an accomplice to Johnson, but did not help him kill Big Frank.

The blood that was found on Winfro Lorenzo Johnson's clothes and Big Frank's body matched. Therefore, he is sentenced to hang by the neck until he is dead. Clarence (Dial) Harris is found to be an accomplice and will serve 1 year and sixty days in the Madison county jail without a chance of parole.

Mrs. Johnson fainted, and mama just moaned and held onto Mr. Curtis. Two of Mrs. Johnson's sons lifted her limp body above the crowd and carried her outside.

The rest of the colored folks walked slowly out of the courthouse back into the rain. The crowd inside cheered until the judge banged so hard that he broke the stick in his hand.

As Mr. Curtis helped mama down the stairs we heard a familiar voice yelling; "Get out of my way dam it". Get out of my way". It was Miss Francine! She was dressed in a red dress, red high-heeled shoes, and a red hat with a feather on top. She looked like the ladies in the magazine at Neuman's store, only brighter. "I said get out of my way! Miss Hattie was running behind her with an umbrella calling for her to stop. But Miss Francine was walking like she had some business to do and no one could stop her.

The crowd parted for her to walk through. Everybody in the crowd turned around and followed Miss Francine back inside the courthouse. They filled the hallway until it felt like it would explode. Miss Francine walked right up to the judge and said if you don't let them go free I promise you as the devil in hell is my witness I will turn this place out. All you high and mighty sons of whores and bitches, I promise I will call every one of you out.

By this time Mr. Rooker had gotten to Miss Francine. He tried to get her to come home with him. Miss Hattie tried to get her to calm down. That didn't happen. Miss Francine turned her wrath on old judge Witherspoon. Damn you Haley James Witherspoon you let these men go or so help me God you will be the first one I turn out. Judge Witherspoon didn't look like the "hanging judge" no more. He looked like Bessie my tabby cat after mama threw water on her on accident, and he was as red as Miss Francine's dress and matching hat.

You could hear a pin fall in that courtroom. Witherspoon looked at the jury and the jury looked at him. Finally the judge hit down the gavel and said; "case dismissed for lack of evidence". The white folks went wild. They yelled and cussed, and threw paper and fans.

Miss Francine screamed and all eyes were fastened on her. She let her head turn around so fast and far that it looked like the red hat with the feather would jump right off her head and poke the first person that moved. With her eyes focused on nearly every body in that courtroom Miss Francine spit the words out of her mouth so strongly that they flew across the room like the b b's from Willie Earl's old b b gun. "Alright now, all of you yelling and screaming come down here right now and let me tell your story for you." spat Miss Francine.

Nobody moved. Finally the white folks found their feet. They started to file out of the courtroom one at a time until there was nobody left but, Judge Witherspoon, Mr. Rooker, Hattie, Miss Francine, and the sheriff. The sheriff took the metal bands off of daddy and Mr. Johnson's arms and legs.

Mama ran to daddy and Miss Francine fell to the floor in what looked like a pile of red blood. She was crying and squirming around. Mr. Rooker tried his best to get her, up but she just screamed louder. Miss Hattie couldn't get her to calm down. Miss Francine just lay there on that wooden floor and cried. She would not be consoled. Mrs. Johnson had come out of her fainting spell. She and all of her children ran to Mr. Johnson.

We all walked out into the muggy, hot night. The rain had stopped and the air was damp and heavy. You could hear the bugs and the crickets, making sounds in the bushes. Mr. Johnson and his family stepped out of the courthouse. Mama and daddy and me came out behind them. A sound like a firecracker rang out so loud that everybody fell to the ground.

Chapter 7

THE JOHNSON FAMILY buried their daddy in the graveyard behind the church, not far from where Willie Earl's grave was. I looked at the stone that was on my brother's grave. Willie Earl Harris, born to Clarence and Beatrice Harris. Tears ran down my face, as I stood there thinking about my dead brother. Lola and her brothers and sisters all cried so hard that it made my heart ache in my chest. I thought my chest would cave in. I went to my friend Lola and squeezed her real hard. I thought about what Rev Tremble said as we walked to the church fellowship hall. "He was a man of sorrows, acquainted with grief". For the first time in my life I understood what that meant. Lola and me were just like Jesus now. We both were acquainted with grief.

The loud ringing noise in the house still scared me. I had not gotten used to the telephone in the house. Miss Francine said every body needed a telephone these days, especially us. With Sammy in the service and mama doing

Miss Francine's laundry, she felt like we needed a telephone. Miss Francine had a telephone put in our house. Not too many people we knew had a phone so it didn't ring often. But when it did it was usually Miss Francine. She always asked for mama, but mama was always at the church these days. Daddy was usually home that time of day. He got off work at the mill everyday at 3 o'clock and came home to take a nap before mama got home. He always ended up having to tend to something for Miss Francine at 4 o'clock every Wednesday.

Mama and the Ladies Aide were busy working on getting things ready for a big surprise for Miss Sutton. Miss Sutton didn't come to school anymore. Lola told me that she saw Miss Sutton at the Big Sun one Friday afternoon. Lola and her family got money from somewhere because her daddy got killed the night the judge let him and my daddy go free. My daddy hasn't been the same since then. "I think my daddy got the "misery" just like what the doctor said mama had when Willie Earl got killed and daddy was in jail.

Lola and her family got groceries and supplies once a month from the Big Sun store, and now Lola had two pair of shoes. I always had two pairs of shoes. I had one pair of shoes for church and one pair for school. Lola used to have one pair of shoes, but now she had two pair just like me. Lola was my best friend.

Lola said Miss Sutton had a gold ring on her finger with a shiny stone and she told all the colored ladies waiting at the bus stop her new name was "Mrs. Eva Solomon". Lola said all the ladies hugged her and asked her when her "little visitor" was coming. By then the bus came and all the colored people got on and went to the back and sat together.

Lola loved riding the bus once a month with all of the other colored folk coming and going to town. Once while riding the bus Lola had her nose pressed to the window glass and she thought she saw Mr. Dial going in the side door of the funeral home. Lola just thought she was seeing things and shrugged it off, because everybody knew the funeral home was closed on Wednesdays' because Mr. Rooker was at his Funeral Director's meeting in Columbus.

Lola said that when she saw Miss Sutton she was real fat. Lola said it was that same fat her mama had when her little brother came to live with them. Lola said she heard her mama and big sisters talking and the said that kind of fat was called "family way." Lola knew they were right because every time she saw her mama and other ladies with that kind of fat a new person came to live with their family and they were always in the way. Whenever Miss Francine called on the phone on Wednesday afternoon's daddy would talk real low on the phone, wash his face and leave the house. That telephone made my whole family act real funny at times.

I went inside and sat on my bed. I was trying to decide whether or not to take the package out from under the bed and open it up. Lola came to the back door and called my name. I let her inside. Lola saw me sit on the bed. "Ooooo." said Lola, your mama gon whip you for sitting on that bed." Lola smiled at me but I didn't smile back. "What's wrong with you?' Lola asked. "Lola, I got something and I'm scared.' I said. "Pookie Harris, you didn't dig up that sack did you?" No, I said, but I got this." I shoved the papers into Lola's hands. Lola looked at the package. What's this?" Lola asked with a puzzled look on her face. "I don't know. I found them behind the kitchen hutch when I was sweeping and I hid it because I didn't know what else to do." I said all in one breath, and I started to cry.

Lola sat on the bed. She stared at the bundle. "What do you want to do Pookie?" Lola asked in a choked whisper." "I don't, I don't know. I feel like it is something bad." Well Pookie, the only way we gon know is to open them, or we can bury them with the sack if you want to." said Lola. "You do it. I can't. Please Lola open them." I said between sobs and tears.

We opened the bundle, saw what was inside, and it changed my whole life. Everyday after school for one month Lola and I explored the bundle. Each day led to new discoveries, new tears, and raw emotions. Lola and I cried for two months as we poured through that bundle.

When I got off of the school bus that afternoon and walked in the house, I heard mama talking on the telephone. She was smiling and crying at the same time. She turned to me and said "guess what? "What?" I asked. "Sammy is coming home." She said. We danced around the room until we heard the front door shut. It was daddy. "What is going on?" he asked.

Mama turned and started to walk into the kitchen and said in a low tone, "Ask Annie." I looked at daddy and the back of mama as she walked into the kitchen and I said, "Sammy is coming home next week." Daddy smiled, rumbled through his pocket, went out onto the porch. He sat down, and found what he was looking for in his pockets. He rolled a cigarette with tobacco from the red can with the man dressed in the funny clothes on the front. The sweet aroma of the tobacco drifted through the air and into the living room where I was standing. I went to my room and changed my clothes so that I could help mama get dinner ready. We ate in silence that night. Each one of us had a mountain of heartache going through our bodies and minds.

Chapter 8

WE WERE SITTING in the living room watching our new television. Daddy was trying to make the rabbit ears stand up. The color paper with the blue and green that was supposed to make the picture colorful always fell off, but it was still fun to watch. We watched "Mickey Mouse" and daddy's favorite "Gun smoke." Daddy said we got our television from Sears Roebuck but Miss Francine had it sent to our house. We were the only colored people in Madison County with a television and a telephone. Folks said we had got to be "uppity negroes."

Daddy finally admitted that the television came from Miss Francine. He said he paid her back by doing odd jobs around the funeral home and Miss Francine's house. Just as daddy got the picture just right someone knocked on the door. I thought it was Lola so I went to let her in. I couldn't believe my eyes. It was Sammy! Sammy looked like Sammy but in a different way. He was taller and wider and he looked more like daddy than he did himself. He had a uniform that was pressed and stiff. He was wearing a hat that he took off the minute he stepped into the house. He picked me up and hugged me real tight and called my name over and over. "Pookie, my Pookie." When he finally put me down he looked at me up and down. "Pookie you all legs now. You grew girl. You really grew." I couldn't speak. Words were in my throat but they wouldn't come out.

Mama and daddy came into the room. Mama ran straight to Sammy. She hugged him and cried so much that when she pulled away Sammy's uniform was all wet across the top. Daddy stood back and just stared at Sammy. Finally, daddy put his hand out and Sammy grabbed it and they shook hands real hard with one hand on top of the other. Daddy and Sammy gazed at each other. Finally daddy said, "welcome home soldier." "Thank you sir." Sammy said with a smile. All of a sudden Sammy fell into daddy's arms and the two men hugged for a long time. Mama went to the kitchen to fix supper for Sammy. Daddy and Sammy talked most of the night. Their talk was different from when Sammy lived at home with us. Sammy finished every sentence with "sir." It was good listening to them talk. Their voices were different now. It was man to man.

Sammy and Pearline got married Saturday afternoon May 15, 1955 at Pearline's parents' house. The house looked beautiful. Miss Viola sang a song I had heard on the radio. Miss Hattie and mama served food on paper plates.

Mrs. Eva Sutton Solomon was sitting in the kitchen nursing her baby boy. He was fat and round and brown. He kicked his legs while he nursed. He was happy, I guess.

Rev Tremble stood up front. Daddy stood next to Sammy. Pearline and her sister marched into the room wearing identical dresses. I heard mama tell Auntie Chauncey that Pearline had to get married at home in an eggshell colored dress because she was already in a family way. Mama said she had counted up the time Sammy came home and how far along Pearline was and it didn't add up. Auntie Chauncey said. "Time will tell. Time will tell."

I sat in the funeral home chairs in the back with Lola. Sammy and Pearline drove around the corner to the house on Merritt Street in Sammy's new car. He got it while he was in the Service. It was green and had shiny black seats. Sammy had decided to stay in the service. Sammy was going to make it his career. I asked daddy what that meant and he said it meant that Sammy wanted to stay in the service for a long time. In one way it made me sad. But if it made Sammy happy then I was happy too.

Sammy and Pearline left Monday morning at 8 o'clock. Mama had packed them some fried chicken, biscuits, cold potato salad, and a jug of iced tea. Mama said it was better than anything they could get on the road. Pearline had spent the night at our house and slept in Sammy and Willie Earl's old room.

Mama had worked hard to make it look nice and bright for Sammy and Pearline. They waved good-bye from the Chevrolet. After that day I didn't see Sammy for a long time.

Chapter 9

J UNIOR HIGH SCHOOL would start in two weeks. Lola and me had spent the whole summer learning to swim at the Center. The center was a place where black kids could go and learn to do all kinds of stuff. We learned to knit, play basketball, baseball, and dance. It was great. I loved swimming best, even though I was not very good at it, like Lola. Lola could glide, float and do a back flip. I did the best I could to get across the pool.

Eighth grade was my best year of school. I was taking art classes. Mrs. Robinson was the art teacher. Mrs. Robinson had a big piece of meat hanging from her face. Lola told me it was a tumor. "Mrs. Robinson had tried to have it cut off lots of times before but it always grew back bigger." Lola told me. I stood there in art class staring at Mrs. Robinson with my mouth hanging open and my eyes bulging out of my head. Lola said that Mrs. Robinson asked me to sit down at least ten times before she finally pulled me into the seat next to her.

Everyday in Mrs. Robinson's class we had to recite the primary colors. When it was time for my row to stand and recite my legs were shaking and my hands were trembling. I opened my mouth to recite the colors and a voice came out that wasn't mine. It was Mrs. Robinson's voice. It was a sloppy swirly kind of voice that sounded like she was holding a gallon of water in that piece of meat on her face.

Lola and I would practice saying our primary colors everyday in the smoke house. Each time that I would recite my colors using Mrs. Robinson's voice Lola would fall on the floor in the smoke house, and roll around in the hay in a fit of laughter. I had to pat her on the back really hard until she stopped choking. The tears would roll down our cheeks like rainwater. We would lie on the floor of the smoke house worn out from laughing so hard.

When I stood to recite my colors that day in the classroom it was as if I was in the smoke house alone with Lola, but I wasn't. I was in the middle of Mrs. Robinson's classroom with twenty-five other children, who all roared with laughter as Mrs. Robinson's sloppy voice came from my mouth. Needless to say, I got the worst whipping of my life when mama found out how I had made the whole class laugh when I had imitated Mrs. Robinson that September afternoon in eighth grade.

After that slip up I had to sweep Mrs. Robinson's back porch and steps the rest of the school year.

Everyday Lola and I would sit in the smoke house after swim class and read the letters that I found that day behind the kitchen hutch. I would read and then Lola would read when I would start to cry. Lola read out loud: "My dearest friend. I know that you don't believe that I love you but I do. I followed you here from Alabama. I gave up my friends and family for you. I don't understand why we can't be together. I will love you always. Francine Myers."

The letters were covered with red lipstick kisses. The letter that made my heart stop was dated August 5, 1936. That was a year after Willie was born and a few years before I was born. It said: "Dearest Friend, I had a baby last night. It was beautiful and brown and had curly black hair. Hattie took it away. She said it had died. I know it didn't die because Hattie always gets money from me to take care of his grave, but She won't ever let me see no grave. Good night my lover."

Oh my Lord, Lola and I were old enough to put two and two together now. It was my daddy's child, and mama knew it. Daddy had started up with Miss Francine again and that is why daddy started to sleep in Sammy's room after he left for the service. Miss Francine had fought so hard for my daddy to go free because she loved him. Willie Earl, Mr. Curtis, Mr. Johnson, Mr. Rooker, Miss Francine, Miss Hattie and mama all knew. Now Lola and I knew.

Willie Earl had made me promise not to tell anybody about the sack. I didn't tell a soul. Lola got the shovel from the shed. I followed her to the edge of the field. We dug up the sack that night. The earth was hard and dry because it had not rained for weeks. The weeds were high on that end of the field and it shielded us from the house and the road. I had kept the weeds back from this spot with tar and oil so that I would always know where the spot was. We took turns digging. We had buried it deep all those years ago, and we were paying for it now.

The burlap sack was just like we left it. We fell back on the ground exhausted. When we caught our breath we opened the sack and saw its contents and cried in confirmed belief. We figured that Mr. Rooker knowing that Frank couldn't read was trying to steal the money. But at the same time Mr. Rooker did not want those papers to fall into the wrong hands. That's why Mr. Rooker wanted everybody dead. They shot Big Frank because they thought he double crossed them and gave the sack to daddy and the other men that night, so when they met up with Frank in the alley after daddy and the other men beat Frank with a paddle on his behind, they shot him in the head.

The blood on your daddy's hand came from the fight they had. Your daddy's blood got on Frank from his cut hands. We read the papers that told about a baby being born and was named Harris Francis. It was the same hand that had written the letters to daddy. I thought back and remembered when Mr. Curtis had come to the house that day and told mama about the sack and how she had screamed and searched the house high and low for that sack. The papers said the child would receive monthly allotments until he was 21 and finished college. The money would be given to Miss Hattie every month and she would deliver it to the child's caretaker. The letter was signed and notarized by Mr. Rooker, owner and proprietor of the Rooker Funeral home. You could have knocked us over with a feather.

Chapter 10

THE YEARS FLEW by. Lola and I graduated from high school in the spring. We wore our white dresses with red corsages, and black patent leather shoes. Sammy and Pearline came with the twins, James and John. Maurva Jean and T-Bo came with their children. Bailey came with his new wife Melba. Bailey was farming fulltime now. Papa had long since passed away. Daddy died last December from the tuberculosis he contracted from working in the funeral home.

Miss Francine had arranged for daddy to work every Wednesday after he left the mill. Daddy would work from 3 o'clock until 11 o'clock. Lola told me that one time she and her brothers were coming back from pulling cane and stopped at the funeral home to take the trash out to the back of the funeral home to be burned and saw daddy sitting on the settee with Miss Francine with a bottle of beer in his hands. I cried for a week after she told me that. Lola apologized over and over for telling me. I told her it wasn't her fault. It was daddy who had hurt us all, especially mama.

I could hear mama crying every night in her room, and hear Daddy snoring in Willie Earl and Sammy's old room. Daddy didn't act like himself anymore. I think Willie Earl's death made all of us different. Mama was so sad. I heard her tell Hattie that she was sorry that daddy was dead but that he had done her wrong. He had disgraced the whole family running around with Miss Francine. He was even meeting her in the broad opened daylight in the funeral home when Mr. Rooker went to his meetings.

Miss Francine and Mr. Rooker opened a new funeral home in South Carolina that could hold ten to twelve bodies at a time. Miss Hattie wrote and told mama all about how well the Rookers were doing. They even had a sitting room that Miss Francine had decorated with fancy furniture and swinging lights. Hattie told mama that now the Rookers had a big house with another maid and a chauffer and she was in charge of both of them. She said the maid and the chauffer were more trouble than they were worth.

Lola met a boy from Macon at the public library one afternoon after school. Lola had gone to Atlanta when we were in seventh grade and gotten her teeth fixed. She had two front teeth that almost looked like the beautiful teeth she had when she was a little girl. They fit so nicely and naturally in her mouth and fit well with her other teeth. She had a beautiful smile again. She could smile now without putting her hand over her mouth. Lola and Jackson started dating during our junior year in high school. Lola got engaged her senior year, and was getting married right after graduation. She had already asked me to stand up with her as her maid of honor.

We went to Atlanta last week and picked out some dresses. There was a lady over there that sewed just for black folks. She had her own store and she fitted the dresses to your body. That made me happy because I had filled out all over. Lola was still slim and tall. I had lots of stuff where stuff shouldn't be.

Lola and I had so much fun trying on dresses. We had lunch at a place called the Rib Shack. It was on a street called Sweet Auburn Avenue. Lola got her hair done while we were in Atlanta. She paid for my hair to get done too. I could not believe how different we looked. We even got shoes to match our dresses. Lola got white satin shoes and I got satin shoes too but they had to be dyed to match my dress. My dress was so beautiful. It was peach colored and had swirls of fabric around the skirt. It looked like cotton candy.

When we got back home Lola invited me to see the house where she and Jackson Brown were going to live. Jackson already lived there because he had a good job and had bought the house using his G I benefits. I had never seen Lola so happy. I was happy for her because Lola was my best friend. We got home late Friday night. We were both exhausted. We slept at my house because there was no one there but mama and me now. We talked late into the night about our childhood and all of our adventures. We both agreed that the bullet that hit her daddy in the chest that night when the judge let the two men go free was meant for my daddy. Folks around town said that Mr. Rooker had hired somebody to kill daddy but the man missed and shot Mr. Johnson instead. The man Mr. Rooker wanted dead was still alive and fooling around with his wife. Of course no one could prove anything. No one dared to say anything because Mr. Rooker was a powerful man and could have had any one of them killed and nothing would be said or done about it.

We got up early the next morning. We ate a light breakfast, and then spent the rest of the morning decorating the church and the fellowship hall. Lola and I finally sat down on the pew to rest. We talked for a long time about our childhood and about all of the things that had happened in Madison County. We cried and held each other tight.

The wedding was beautiful. Lola was beautiful. She had tiny flowers in her new hairdo. She was wearing a pearl necklace and tiny pearl earrings. All of Lola's sisters and brothers had come for the wedding. Two of them were bridesmaids. One of her brothers was an usher. The cake was tall and had creamy filling inside. Lola had little napkins that said Lola and Jackson Brown. Lola and Jackson left for their honeymoon in a car filled with crepe paper and rice. Someone had put a sign on the back that said, "Just married." I cried behind my bouquet of calla lilies and white roses, but they were all tears of joy and sweet memories of the times that Lola and I spent together.

I walked up the hill to the house on Merritt Street. I had to get in the house and get busy because tomorrow was a big day for me.

I packed the last of my things in Sammy's old trunk. Mama fixed me a lunch to eat on the bus. I had $12.00 in my purse that the church had collected for me. That money had to last until I got paid from my new job at Maurva Jean's bookkeeping office.

Sammy sent my bus ticket last week from North Carolina where he and Pearline lived with their twin boys. He couldn't get away but he promised to come and visit when I got settled in with Maurva Jean, T Bo and their kids.

"Well." mama said, "This is it." We walked the 6 blocks to the bus station. We hugged and kissed, and said good-bye. I told mama to take good care of herself and Auntie Chauncey. She said she would. We waved each other out of sight.

I was going off to college. I had received a scholarship to Tuskegee Institute in Alabama. Maurva Jean and T-Bo said I could stay with them while I got my degree. I had learned to type in high school so Maurva got me a job at her bookkeeping office. I had gone to visit the office one time last year. It was filled with noisy machines and people dressed in nice clothes, with matching shoes. The men were handsome and smiled at me as Maurva Jean showed me around. Mama moved in with Auntie Chauncey and they organized the first NAACP in Madison County, Georgia, and at last count they had 66 members. I realized as I rode the bus to Alabama that people come and go but friendships last forever. Or so I thought.

PART II

Chapter 1

MY FIRST YEAR at college was hard and fun. I met lots of interesting people from other states. They told some of the best stories that I had ever heard. The girls looked very different from me, and the girls back home. They had straight hair, red lipstick, high-heeled shoes, tight skirts, and even tighter sweaters. I really missed Lola and home.

I had just finished my biology class. I started walking across the Tuskegee campus. There were kids everywhere. The weather was just beginning to change and the leaves were orange and green. I kicked them with my feet as I hurried to the science building to meet with my professor. I was nervous, and my hands shook as I pushed the heavy door back and found myself standing face to face with a lady that looked like Miss Viola but in a different more worldly way. She had glasses with little shiny chips around the edges. Her glasses were shaped like triangles, and they had a long silver chain hanging from one end. Her fingernails were painted bright red, and her hair was piled high on her head like cotton candy.

I stood there and studied her until she looked up and smiled at me and said," Yes, may I help you honey?" I found my voice and said, "Yes ma'am. I am supposed to meet with Dr. Morgan at 2:30. "And just who are you?" asked the woman behind the big wooden desk, in a pleasant tone. "Annie" I squeaked out. "Yes, Annie Harris" I said, as if I didn't know my own name. "Well have a seat Miss Harris. I will let Dr. Morgan know that you are here." The pleasant woman said. She was wearing a slim black skirt, a white blouse with ruffles, and a patent leather belt with matching patent leather shoes. She was very fashionable. I sat down in one of the big soft crimson colored chairs in the large dark room. The rug was crimson with gold swirls. The heavy drapes were crimson with gold stripes. It was a beautiful room. The furniture was all dark wood with little gold knobs and buttons around the edges and drawers.

The lady clicked the box on her desk and spoke into it. "Dr. Morgan," "Yes. Helen." answered the voice from the box. I could tell that it was Dr. Morgan's voice because it had the same deep rich sound that I had gotten used to in biology class. "A Miss Harris is here to see you." Helen said. "Send her in.," the voice answered back. "Yes sir", the woman said into the box. She turned to me and said, "Come with me." I followed her to the wooden door and watched her as she tapped lightly on the door. "Come in," said the voice. Helen stepped aside and nodded for me to go in.

I walked into the room and as I looked around I saw a wall from ceiling to floor filled with books, and pictures, and certificates. There were pictures of children, old people, women, places that had beautiful homes and cars. I stood staring at all of the things in the room. Dr. Morgan motioned to the chair for me to have a seat. My eyes soaked in the atmosphere of the room. The plate on his desk had his name engraved on it with lots of letters behind it. Dr. Abraham Clark Morgan, BS, and MS and PH.D I had heard the other professors when they came into the lab and talked to him. They called him "A C." Some of them called him "doc". He was a very important man at Tuskegee. His door had his name on it, and he was the chairman of the department.

Dr. Morgan was a tall handsome man with wavy hair and big brown eyes. He always wore bow ties and white shirts. His suits were always nicely pressed and fit him like someone had made them just for him. His shoes were always shined. His shoes always made me think of my brother Willie Earl, and the way he took so much pride in the shoes he shined and how they looked when he finished with them.

Dr. Morgan sat with his legs crossed in the big black chair, leaned back, and puffed on his long stemmed pipe. He motioned again for me to sit in the chair with the high back directly in front of his desk. As I sat down I felt my body being enveloped into the velvet cushions. Just as I sat down the phone rang. He answered and talked in whispered tones. I sat and studied him as he talked. He must be about the same age my daddy was when he died of tuberculosis some time back. His hands looked soft and his fingers were long and thin. He looked like he never used his hands except to hold a fountain pen or write on the blackboard in biology class. He swiveled around in his chair and I could see the round spot in his hair where it was thinning out.

Dr. Morgan picked up a paper from his desk and read a list of names from the paper. I heard my name as he read the list. Dr. Morgan hung up the phone. He turned and asked me how I was and how I liked his class. I answered him politely, but I felt a funny sensation in my stomach as I talked to him. It was different than any feeling that I had ever had before. It was different than the feeling that I got when I first turned into a "lady" as mama had said. My period had started the first summer that Lola and I took swim lessons. It was a funny feeling but not like this one.

I remember having a similar feeling once in high school when Lola and I went to the prom and danced with boys for the first time. I danced with a boy named Dallas Richards. He held me so tightly that I could feel his pants get warm and tight on my legs as we moved around the floor. That gave me the same sort of feeling that I was having now. I liked listening to Dr. Morgan's voice. It was smooth and easy. Sometimes in class I listen to his voice, but I don't hear his words. "Miss Harris, Miss Harris," I jumped back to the present. "Did you understand what I said?" asked Dr. Morgan. "Oh I am sorry sir. I was admiring your office, and got lost in my thoughts." I lied. " You have been nominated for a scholarship for next year. "Based on your grades and dedication to your biology labs, we, that is, the biology department has agreed that you should receive a full scholarship next year. The scholarship that you have now will end next year. That means that this scholarship will come just in time. It includes room and board. You can stay on campus and not worry about staying late in the lab" Dr. Morgan said. I could not believe it. I could stay on campus. I could have fun with the others without worrying about catching the last cab to Maurva Jean and T Bo's house. I thanked Dr. Morgan over and over and shook his hand so hard that he moved it back when I tried to shake it again. I ran down the stairs and out of the doors of the science building.

Chapter 2

I WALKED ALL THE way downtown to the bookkeeping office where I worked. It was busy, papers were everywhere, and people seemed to be in a panic. It seems that the federal government was getting ready to audit one of our biggest client's books and everyone was in a tizzy getting ready. When I went to share the news about my scholarship with Maurva she was so busy that she barely responded. "That is great lil sis" she said, and turned away when our boss, Mr. Calloway called her.

I sat down at my desk in the back of the office by the big picture window. My typewriter, my hole puncher, and stapler were all in place, along with a stack of papers that needed to be typed and mailed out today. I got busy typing and humming to myself. The boy who made deliveries on his bicycle for our office came and sat on the trashcan that he turned upside down to sit on when he talked to me.

He always parked his bike at my window and made faces at me while he put his bike in the rack by the window.

I usually pretend not to see him. He would tap on the glass until he got my attention and insisted that I wave at him.

He was cute and friendly, and he was always asking me to go out. I always told him how busy I was, and never went out with him. He took his normal seat on the can and began to tell me about how somebody in the office had made a big mistake with the Gilbert account, and how Mr. Calloway was going to fire whoever it was that made the big mistake.

"Well," he said. "It's Friday night, how about that movie and hamburger?" I opened my mouth to say no and he said" Don't say how busy you are. It's Friday night no classes tomorrow." Yes, I said, but I have labs." "Yeah, yeah, I am gonna have a complex in a minute if you keep saying that. "Please, please Miss Annie Harris, will you go out with me? I promise I am not a serial killer. I am a nice boy from Mississippi, working my way through Tuskegee Institute. Someday when I am a big time agricultural engineer you might wish you had gone out with me." He wore me down. "Okay, I said, I might have some extra time on Saturday night. "Yes! I will pick you up at 7:00. Wear comfortable shoes and save your appetite." he said and ran out before I could say anything.

I finished up my work, and walked back to the lab to complete my project. My lab partner was there. She was putting the finishing touches on our work. "Hello Cathy" I said as I walked in the room. Cathy looked over her horned rimmed glasses and smiled. The gap between her front teeth reminded me of Lola when we were children. Her teeth were white and shiny. Her hair was always pressed and flipped up in the back. She wore her bangs clipped close to her forehead. She always wore jumpers, and white blouses. Her penny loafers were scruffy and never polished. She wore her bobby socks turned down twice. Her headbands always matched her jumpers. People always got us mixed up. I couldn't figure out why because I never wore my hair down. I always wore my hair in a ponytail with a ribbon. My socks were only rolled down once, and I didn't wear glasses. But people always called me Cathy and called Cathy Annie. Needless to say we were both upset about it. We did not get along too well, and never spoke outside of the lab. Cathy was a biology major who always talked about Howard University. She had one more year at Tuskegee and had gained early acceptance into Howard University Medical School. She was my biology mentor.

Cathy Lawson and Dr. Morgan had a close relationship. He would come into the lab and eventually they would end up in his lab office. I never waited around for her after the first time he came to the lab. It was almost an hour later when they came out, and they both looked shocked to see me. They were trying to act casual but it was obvious something was not quite right with them. I gathered my things and left the science building.

I walked home that night, because I needed to clear my head. It was a disturbing picture that I couldn't get out of my mind. Making good grades was my only concern in biology. Dr. Morgan said "I had a good head on my shoulders, and that I needed to expose myself to all the library material that I could." "He would always say," Try your best to follow in

Cathy Lawson's footsteps. She is a fine student and a true credit to the university." I tried hard but Cathy never let me get close to her. Whenever I would try to talk to her she would always stop in the middle of the conversation and say that she had to leave. Eventually I stopped trying. I talked it over with Maurva Jean one night and she said "Some people are just quiet that way, Annie, Don't take it personal. It's just her way. Try talking to her again later. Maybe she has a lot on her mind, what with trying to get into Howard. I hear that's a tough school. Anyway keep trying. Remember, everybody is not as talkative or as pretty as you are." I left it at that. Maurva had made her point. I wasn't going to press the issue of Cathy Lawson. She went her way and I went mine.

Saturday night came fast. I still had not decided what to wear on my so-called date with Mark Allen. He had said to wear comfortable shoes. I was so hungry because I had not eaten all day. I had gone to the lab early that morning to get some work done. Mark had said to save my appetite. I was starving by the time Mark got to my house. He was dressed so neatly. He had a white shirt with a bow tie. His hair was shiny with waves. His small moustache was neatly trimmed. He was wearing a black sweater and khaki pants with a brown leather belt. His chest muscles rippled under the sweater, and the muscles in his arms flexed every time he moved. His loafers had tassels, and had a shine on them that would have made Willie Earl proud. His jacket had designs and emblems all over it. I didn't know what they meant, but I knew that the letters were Greek The way he turned his head and held his body erect reminded me of Sammy when he was in high school.

I was wearing a mint green dress with little pink flowers. I had my pink sweater with the gold clasp that Maurva had given me for my birthday. I had washed my hair and Maurva had pressed it for me. I had shined my patent leather pumps with a left over biscuit like I had been taught as a child growing up in Georgia. When we were walking out the door T-Bo said, "hey man, that's our baby sister." Mark and T-Bo let a look pass between them that I had seen pass between daddy and Sammy plenty of times when Sammy and Pearline would go out on Sunday afternoons to the movies.

I was expecting to walk to wherever we were going because I had only seen Mark riding his bike to work. When we rounded the corner of the house I saw a black car behind T-Bo's truck. As we walked to the car I was shocked when Mark took me by the arm and led me to the passenger's side. He opened the door and I stood there for a second in amazement. He nudged my elbow and said, "Get in. It's safe." I got in and looked around inside of the car. It was clean and smelled like leather and wood. There was a funny looking medallion hanging from his dashboard. It had an odd shape. Mark cranked the car and we drove off.

When we pulled into the colored section of the drive in Mark bought our tickets. I offered to pay for mine but he pretended to be insulted and pushed my hand away. It was a great movie. It was called Paris Blues. Mark said he had read the book in high school. It starred the two new colored actors Sidney Poitier and Diahann Carroll. We left the movie and drove to the Purple Onion. There were kids everywhere. The music was blaring and people were dancing inside and outside. We finally found a table. Mark told me all about the food. He helped me order. We both had the "Tall Burger." We shared fries. We each had a milkshake. Again, I offered to pay but Mark said, "No, I wouldn't ask you out if I didn't have money. His tone and facial expression let me know how hurt he was. "I know," I said apologetically. "I just want to do my share." I said apologetically. Mark and I sat and talked for about 2 hours. He told me all about his life in Mississippi. His mother is a teacher and his father owned a mechanic shop. He told me about his sister who was a pre-med student at Howard. He said his sister was very smart and had gotten full scholarships to Tuskegee and Howard. She had married a boy from Africa and they had planned to go back to Africa and practice medicine. Mark's mom taught science at the local high school for the last 27 years, and planned to retire when Mark finished school. He told me that his mom met his dad and after they got married she put up the money for his mechanic shop. They had three other mechanics working for them. Mark and his family were rich compared to my family and me.

We sat there until 11:oclock. I didn't realize it was so late as I glanced at the wristwatch I had bought for myself with my first paycheck from my job at the book keeping shop. "I hope you had a good time," Mark said. " I did," I said as we walked to the car. There were kids everywhere kissing and pressed hard against each other on the back and sides of cars. "What is going on?" I asked. Mark looked at me and winked. "I think it looks like fun" he said. You want to try it"? I didn't say anything as Mark let me in the car, closed the door, and walked quickly to the other side. He slid under the wheel and we drove in silence for a while. When we reached the house Mark turned to me, and I felt queasy. I didn't know if it was the hamburger or my nerves. Mark spoke in a tone I wasn't familiar with. It was breathless and heavy. "I 'm sorry if I offended you back there. I was only joking. Please forgive me. I wouldn't want to do anything to upset you Annie." Mark spoke in breathless tones. He sounded the way he did when he ran in from his bike route, only in a more quiet way. "Oh no," I said. You were fine. I really had a good time." We better go in. It's late. I said sleepily. Mark Allen walked me to the door. I looked for my key in my purse. I finally found them. Mark took the keys from my hand and unlocked the front door. T-Bo was sitting in the living room. He was looking through a magazine. "Hello" he said cheerily. Did you guys have a good time? Mark spoke up and said, "Yes, it was cool, Annie is a good listener. I think I nearly talked her ear off" Mark said casually. "Well good night Annie. I had a good time. Goodnight everyone. See you tomorrow." With that Mark was out of the front door. I could hear his footstep as he walked to his car. I heard the engine as he drove off. When I turned around T-Bo was studying the magazine and Maurva Jean walked in from the kitchen. "Hey baby girl. Did you have a good time"? She asked sweetly. "Yes, I said. It was great. I am going to bed. Goodnight Maurva, T-Bo."

I walked to my room thinking about the night. I really did have a good time. Mark Allen was a nice person. He was not at all like the messenger boy I saw at work everyday. I pulled the nightgown over my head, covered myself with the patch quilt and fell asleep.

I heard Maurva calling me. It seemed like my head had just touched the pillow. "Annie, Annie, get up we are going to be late for church. I struggled to get out of bed. I hurried to the bathroom, and got myself ready for church. I didn't have time to eat, so I drank some orange juice and ran out of the door. Maurva and T-Bo and the babies were already in the car and ready to go. I sat in the backseat with the children. It was my job to keep them quiet during the ride and in church. When we got to church the choir was already in the choir stand, and singing. We sat in the next to the last pew because we were late, and because if the children got restless we could ease out without disturbing other people. The church was full of college kids that I knew. I saw Dr. Morgan on the second pew, and the woman next to him looked familiar. I couldn't remember where I had seen her before. As I sat there my mind drifted off to the night before. Mark Allen was really fun, and such a nice person. I never thought that he could be so polite. He knew so much about many things. I was fascinated by his knowledge of everything. We talked about his career and agricultural engineering. He wanted to help make agriculture better for the farmers across the world. Then I remembered where I had seen the woman next to Dr. Morgan. She was in the picture on his desk. There were two teenage kids next to the woman. I think they were probably his kids.

The preacher's voice made me jump back to reality as he ended his sermon. There were special announcements and a celebration in the fellowship hall. Maurva and T-Bo nodded for me to come with them out of the door. I gathered up the children and we slid out of the side door. As I stepped out of the door I walked right into Mark Allen. He was dressed in a very nice suit with a gold necktie with the same design as the symbol hanging from his dashboard in his car. "Hello" he said. "Let me help you. You seem to have your hands full." I felt embarrassed as I stumbled along with the children. Mark got a hold of Lester Lee's hand, and I got a hold of Little Bea.

Tammy walked on ahead of us. She was twelve, and tall for her age. She was smart in school and loved reading books. She stayed in her room most of the time and read books all day when her school was out for a holiday. When we finally got to the car T-Bo and Maurva Jean were already there. T-Bo teased Mark, "What took you so long?" "Well I kinda had my hands full." Mark said, and winked and smiled at all of us. As we got into the car Maurva said over her shoulder, "Come on over to the house for dinner. We got fried chicken." Mark looked at me, and I smiled my "It's okay" smile. He said, "Yes, I would like that." Mark got into his car and drove behind us the short distance to the house.

We finished dinner and Mark and I volunteered to clean up the kitchen. We washed everything in sight. Mark held my hand under the soapy water. It felt nice. Mark stepped back from the sink and dried his hands on the dishtowel. He looked at me with a strange expression on his face. He said, "I am going to marry you Annie Harris." I said, Mark Allen, you don't even know me." Mark stared at me with a dreamy look in his eyes and said. "I know you well enough to know that I want to marry you."

I walked away from him and went to the window. There were chickens in the yard, and a goat with three legs. I looked at them and wondered about how to answer Mark without hurting his feelings. "Mark, I said, as I turned around to face him "I want to finish college. I want to get my degree and work." As I stared at him I could see his eyes dancing. They were dancing the same way that they did at the bookkeeping office when he teased me while sitting on the trash can at my desk. "Not now, knuckle head," he said while trying not to laugh. "I mean after college, you know when we both finish up." "Oh" I said, looking embarrassed. "In that case, let's finish the dishes." We have a little more time before that happens." I breathed a sigh of relief.

Maurva walked in just then and said, that they were all going to the park for the music concert. She asked if we wanted to come along. We both said no at the same time. Mark and I both had class work to do. I had to get to the lab, and he had a paper to finish. Mark left with the others. I changed my clothes and went to the lab.

Chapter 3

IT WAS QUIET and dark. I walked in and I could hear voices in Dr. Morgan's lab office. He usually had students in his office discussing their lab projects and grades. These voices sounded different. It took me a minute but I finally figured out the other voice. It was Cathy Lawson's voice. Their voices were loud and it sounded like two people arguing. I started to put my lab coat on but I changed my mind. I got my things and started to leave when the office door opened and I heard Cathy Lawson's voice scream out, "You low down dirty bastard. You will pay for this. Just you wait and see." The door slammed and it made me jump. Before I could get out of the front door my eyes met Cathy's. They were flooded with tears and fiery with what seemed liked hurt and anger all mixed together. I tried to say something but the words came out all jumbled. Cathy rushed past me, out the front door, and down the stairs. I stood there with my lab coat in my hand and my mouth open. I was embarrassed for her and sorry that I had heard anything.

I walked slowly home. I left the lab soon after Cathy. I knew that I couldn't stay in the lab and run the risk of Dr. Morgan seeing me. That would be too awkward and embarrassing for both of us. The things that I heard them say to each other kept running through my brain. Cathy said she was six weeks. Dr. Morgan replied, "take the name of this place, and get out of here." When I got home no one was there. I tried to study in my room but I needed my notes and my materials. They were all in the lab. I waited an hour and then I went back to the lab. I wanted to make sure everyone was gone before I went back.

As I walked up the hill I saw T-Bo's car coming down the hill. He blew the horn at me and I waved at them. When I got to the lab it was dark and the door was locked. I dug in the flowerpot on the porch until I found the key. I unlocked the door and went to my desk. I opened my notebook and started to work.

I heard someone moving around. I looked up and saw the light coming from under the door of Dr. Morgan's office. "Oh no, I thought he was gone," I said under my breath. Just as I got up to leave, the office door opened and I was caught like a fox in the hen house. "Miss Harris, you should have made your presence known," Dr. Morgan said in his rich deep voice. "Oh I am sorry sir I didn't know that anyone else was here." I said nervously as I fumbled with my lab coat. "The door was locked and I let myself in. I didn't know anyone was here." I said in a trembling voice.

"Oh no, he said. "It is fine?" Did you just arrive?" Yes sir,"
I mumbled. "Well finish up your work and lock up when
you are done," he said as he eyed me suspiciously. "Have you
seen your lab partner today" he asked in a fake casual tone.
"No sir" I lied. I just wanted him to go. I wanted to tell him
that I had heard his conversation but that his secret was safe
with me. "Well, have a good evening," he said as he walked
through the door and closed it behind him.

Monday morning came too quickly, and I had lost
too much time this weekend. I wasn't prepared for class.
I handed in a half done lab report. Dr. Morgan didn't say
anything. He just gave me a funny look. My history class
was no better. I made a C on the mid-term. The last few
weeks were awful for me. I couldn't seem to get it together.

I walked to the lab to check on my project and pick-up
my notes. I walked in the lab to find Cathy Lawson bent
over the trashcan heaving and sighing. I rushed over to help
her but she pushed me away. "Leave me alone she shouted
between gags. I ignored her and helped her to stand up. She
was shaking, heaving, and crying all at once. I helped her to
the couch where we laid out our lab reports. I pushed them
to the floor and helped her lie down. I got a wet towel from
the restroom for Cathy to wipe across her face. I helped her
get herself together. She cried for about half an hour. I held
her in my arms and tried to soothe her broken spirit. Finally
she started to talk. She told me that she had been seeing Dr.
Morgan. They had had an affair and now she was pregnant.
It all came over me like a flood of cold water. It was obvious

as to what the shouting and argument was about that day when I walked in on them in the lab.

It was obvious that Cathy was telling him her condition and the solution he was offering was unbearable to all who heard it. "What am I going to do?" Cathy wailed. I didn't know what to say. I just sat there dumbfounded. Cathy sat up and pulled a big wad of money from underneath her sweater. I had noticed that Cathy's clothes had become bigger and looser these days, and now I knew why. "He wants me to have the baby killed she wailed." I don't know what to do. My parents will kill me if they ever found out. What will I do about my scholarship, and school next fall? What am I going to do?" she yelled. I had to have time to think. I had never had to face a problem like this before. I told Cathy to come home with me tonight and we could work something out. "No", she moaned. "This is my problem and I have to work it out on my own." she said. "Cathy", I said. "Let me help you. I am here for you. I am your friend." Cathy finally got up and cleaned herself up. We straightened up the lab, locked the door and walked to my house.

It was late and the kids were in bed. Maurva and T-Bo were watching television with the lights out. Cathy and I walked in. It was a good thing that it was dark in the room because we were a mess from our afternoon lab experience. I introduced Cathy to them, and told them we had a big exam tomorrow, and we were going to study most of the night. Maurva said okay in a sleepy voice, and told me that I had some mail from home on the dresser. We all said good night. I finally convinced Cathy that everything would be okay. She took a shower, and I gave her some pajamas. She was slow about accepting anything and kept questioning me about why I wanted to help her. I told her that was what friends did for one another. She argued that she hardly knew me. I told her we would fix that real soon.

Cathy fell asleep the minute her head hit the pillow. I stayed up and read the mail from home. I started with the letter from mama first. She said "all was well, except Miss Viola had a stroke, but everyone was pitching in to help her, and she was improving everyday". Mr. Neuman had passed away and his sons had taken over the store. Mama said, "They were not nice like their father, and had made everyone pay off their credit bill" she went on. "Sammy and his family were doing well and he would write me soon." "See you soon, Love, Mama." I flipped over the pile of mail and at the bottom was a letter from Lola. Lola was my best friend. My hands trembled as I opened the letter.

Dear Annie,

I hope that this letter finds you well. I have missed you so much. I am coming for a visit next week. We have so much to talk about and catch up on. I can't wait to see you. Please meet me at the bus depot at 6pm Thursday, the 15th I can't wait to see you.

Love to all, Lola.

It was a letter from my best friend Lola. It was written in the beautiful handwriting that I remembered from third grade. Lola was coming to visit. Lola was my best friend. My mind drifted away from the present, and back to when

Lola and I were little girls hiding under the bed at mama's house. Cathy moaned loudly in her sleep, and my mind came quickly back to the situation at hand. Lola was coming and she would help me solve this problem, just as she always did when we were little girls. I could hardly wait for next Thursday the 15th.

Chapter 4

MARK ALLEN WAS pacing up and down the sidewalk looking at his watch. The Purple Onion was packed with students. Annie was late and Mark was not very patient with people who were late. He loved Annie and they had been dating steadily for a while. He had finally convinced her to let him kiss her. Since that first kiss he had become consumed with Annie. They had done a little heavy petting but that was as far as it had gone. Annie was adamant about that. He had learned to adjust. Mark was used to fast girls who would basically do his bidding. But Annie was different. She was the girl he wanted to marry. He handled Annie like she was a beautiful precious flower. But he had the feeling that Annie didn't feel as deeply about him as he felt about her. But he was willing to wait as long as needed to have Annie.

I was rushing to the bus station to meet Lola. I had completely forgotten to tell Mark what day Lola was coming. I also did not share Cathy's secret with him or anyone else because Cathy had made me swear not too tell anyone. This put an added strain on my relationship with Mark. I was always making excuses for not meeting him when I was supposed to. It was getting harder to disguise Cathy's condition. I felt like I was on a roller coaster that was spinning out of control and I wanted to get off.

I was trying to juggle school, lab, and work at the bookkeeping office with Mark and Cathy. Something had to give. Mark was unintentionally placed on the back burner. I was spending a lot of time in Cathy's dorm room because she was always sick. I had told Maurva that Cathy and I were lab partners and it was a lot easier for me to stay with Cathy because she was living on campus, and it was easier to get to the dorm from the lab when we had late sessions. It wasn't really a lie, but it wasn't quite the truth.

The bus came in right on time. I searched frantically for Lola through the windows with my eyes as the bus rolled to a stop, and spewed hot air all around me. My eyes finally rested on who I believed to be Lola. Lola had gotten her front teeth fixed when we were in junior high. Her beautiful smile had been restored, but Lola's mouth had not changed. She still had the full round lips, and the bright pink gums. When the girl on the bus turned around and smiled I realized that it was not Lola. As I turned and started to walk around to the other side of the bus I heard someone call out "Pookie". It was a sound that I had not heard in months, and it was music to my ears. "Lola, oh my goodness, Lola." Was all I could manage to say. The tears rolled down our cheeks and intermingled with each other's. We hugged and tasted the sweet saltiness of the other's tears as we felt a lifetime of friendship pass between us.

Lola and I walked to Maurva's house. We walked through town. I showed Lola the sights and popular places in town. We headed up the hill towards the campus. As we walked I recognized a figure standing in front of the Purple Onion. "Oh my goodness" I shouted out and grabbed my face. Lola looked at me and grabbed my hand. "What's the matter Pookie" she asked nervously. "Nothing, I oh lord, what am I going to do?" I said half to myself and half out loud.

Mark had been more than patient with me these last few days. I don't know what to do. I thought to myself, as we got closer to him. Mark turned and saw us. As we got closer to him he turned and glared at me and walked quickly away, got in his car, and sped off. "Who was that?' Lola asked. "Oh just somebody I know." I lied. "Oh, Lola said with her eyes stretched wide, and that big wide grin. "He sure was good-looking. We finally reached the house. When we got to the front door Maurva and T-Bo welcomed Lola with opened arms because they know how much Lola meant to me. We sat down to a wonderful dinner that T-Bo had cooked. He was a great cook, and did most of the cooking in the house. T-Bo had barbequed ribs, made potato salad, baked beans, and lemon pie. It was wonderful and we all ate too much. Maurva told us to go on and get Lola settled in. She and the children would clean up. T-Bo had his lodge meeting, and some work he had to finish in the garage.

We went into the bedroom and Lola sat down in the old rocking chair in the room. "I love this room." Lola said as she got up and walked around and explored every nook and cranny. "Can you hide under this bed?" she teased. We both laughed, and started talking about her marriage, and home in Georgia.

Lola explained about how she and Jackson really loved each other very much, but there was something wrong with her. "Every time Jackson tries to make love to me I get nervous and jittery." Lola explained with tears and eyes that screamed out help. "I try very hard Annie, and Jackson has been so patient with me. He thought it was because I was a new bride and a virgin." "Oh Pookie, I don't know what to do. I love my husband. I just don't know what to do." Lola said miserably. I stood there frozen. As Lola talked about how night after night they tried, but got nowhere I didn't know what to say. I began to think back to when we were little. I remember how badly Big Frank had hurt Lola when we were kids. The doctor at that time had said that Lola would be fine in time. I thought that she was. When I found my voice, I asked Lola" have you she seen a doctor?" "Yes, I went to the doctor on the base where Jackson had been stationed in the service." Lola said. " He said I was fine. "Lola, did you tell Jackson what happened?" I asked. "Oh Pookie, I couldn't tell him that. He would never want to have anything to do with me if he knew that." I took

Lola by the hand and we walked over to the bed. I sat down and patted for Lola to sit next to me. She looked reluctant because as kids we were never allowed to sit on the bed. I flipped back the covers and Lola slowly sat down.

Chapter 5

CATHY WALKED AROUND in her dorm room in deep thought. She pulled out the papers that Dr. Morgan had given her. They had the name and address of the people that could "take care of the situation" as he so tactfully put it that day in his lab office.

Cathy had come all the way from Cleveland, Ohio to attend Tuskegee Institute. She had heard so much about the school when she was growing up. Cathy was a smart girl. She had worked really hard in school. At graduation time she received several scholarship offers. But, her heart was set on Tuskegee. One of her high school teachers had gone there and had met with Dr. Booker T. Washington, and Dr. G.W. Carver. They were both great scholars. Dr Carver was a famous scientist. Cathy wanted to be a famous scientist just like him. She had done many experiments in high school. She had garnered a reputation as one of finest young minds at the Frederick Douglas High School in Cleveland. Cathy was the oldest in her family and was expected to help her younger brother and sister. Cathy was determined to do just that. No one was going to stop her and destroy her dream.

Dr. A. C. Morgan had befriended Cathy when she got to Tuskegee over three years ago. He had taken a special interest in her because he said;" She had a good mind." Cathy had fallen hard for Dr. Morgan. They had spent many nights locked away in the lab. He was charming, sophisticated, and not at all like the country boys in Cleveland Ohio. She would eat and sleep in the lab waiting for him. She had learned to do research very well and did much of Dr. Morgan's personal research when he was finishing up his doctorate degree. He had promised to get her into Howard University's Medical School when she finished Tuskegee. Cathy noticed that things had started to change when Dr. Abraham B. Morgan received the chairmanship of the Biology Department. He spent less time with her. He hardly ever came to the lab. When he did come he was always busy with other students. He barely spoke to her. Cathy was not the kind of girl that would roll over and play dead. She had a plan. She was thinking of a way to carry out that plan.

Cathy had decided to go and visit the place that Dr. Morgan had insisted that she see.

The afternoon bus to Haleyville would be leaving in about thirty minutes. She had time to go by the lab and take care of some last minute things before catching the bus. The roundtrip fare was six dollars. She had plenty of money. Dr. Morgan had seen to that. Cathy packed a lunch, changed hr clothes and left the dorm. When she got to the lab it was locked. Cathy let herself in and took care of the things she needed to and left for the bus station. Cathy hated the bus. She had ridden the bus to Tuskegee from Cleveland. She had never gone back. She explained to her family that she had a job and it required her to work weekends and holidays, and there was no time left to come home. She had very little contact with her parents because her father worked 16 hours at the car plant, and her mother worked for Sears Roebuck as a window changer. They had little time for writing or anything else except to take care of her younger brother and sister.

As the bus pulled into the station the fumes made Cathy nauseous, as did everything else these days. Cathy boarded the bus along with the others. She sat down midway of the bus, next to the window. The bus ride was short, only forty minutes. Cathy got off the bus and pulled out the papers with the name of the place and the street where it was located. Cathy stopped at a gas station and asked for directions. The white men looked at her and sneered. They pointed in the direction of a clump of trees and instructed her to go between the grove of trees and the place she was looking for would be on her right.

Cathy observed her surroundings. The trees had strings of moss and dead branches hanging off of them. The dirt road looked dark and scary. There were people walking along that looked like they were lost and homeless. Cathy finally found the place. It had windows covered with tin foil. It looked run down and dilapidated. Cathy knocked on the door. A voice said come in. Cathy's eyes had to adjust to the dark room. When her eyes finally focused she observed that the inside was worse than the outside. The room was dark and smelled awful. A big fat woman came from between some curtains that were made from bed sheets, and slung over what looked like the branch of a tree. There were candles burning and the odor was awful. Cathy got sick while sitting in the chair. She started to vomit and the woman handed her a bucket. Cathy wretched and heaved for about five minutes before she could sit up again.

The fat woman asked her if she had the 150.00 for the "elimination" Cathy reached inside the pocket of her jacket and counted out the money. Cathy thought about the word elimination over and over again. The fat woman beckoned for her to come with her behind the curtain made of bed sheets. Cathy got up and walked towards the opening. She stepped into what looked like a makeshift hospital room. Cathy recognized the smells immediately because of her work in the lab. The smell of formaldehyde, alcohol, were all familiar to her, but the other things she saw made her take a step backwards. There were what looked like used needles on a table. Cathy thought about how the needles looked similar to the ones some of the veterinary students used in the lab on the animals. There was a stove with a huge black pot of boiling water sitting on it. The fat woman told her to take her clothes off. As Cathy began to take off her coat she saw a very small woman come into the room wearing a rubber apron and rubber gloves. The fat woman picked up a handful of knives, a large spoon, and several other small instruments from a table on the other side of the room and brought them over and threw them into the pot of boiling water on the stove.

~

Lola sat on the bed with Annie and poured her heart out about her inability to make love with her husband, Jackson. "Lola, you have to be honest with Jackson, I said sympathetically. "You have to tell him everything. If he really loves you he will try his best to work it out with you." I said. "Oh Pookie, I love you so much. Maybe, I could do that. In the meantime let's spend this week just catching up and remembering good times spent on Merritt Street." Lola said sweetly. " That's fine but I have some lab work to do and I have someone that I want you to meet." I said. "Come on, go wash your face and freshen-up. I know how the bus rides can be." I said, as we laughed and went together just like old times to wash-up together.

We walked out into the bright sun and towards the dorms and the campus. I pointed out some of the sights to Lola, and she was amazed at how many students were on the campus, and at the way they dressed. As we approached Cathy's dorm room I explained to Lola briefly about Cathy's situation, and how she had eventually opened up to me and told me the whole story. "Cathy has made me promise not to tell anything to anyone, so I can only tell you enough to make you understand how sensitive the situation is." I told Lola intimately. "I know Annie, we have shared so many things over the years that I dare not tell anyone anything about what we talk about." Lola said earnestly.

I opened the door to the dorm room. Cathy was not there. Things were scattered about as if someone had left in a hurry. I had a funny feeling. I looked in the drawer where Cathy kept the roll of money that Dr. Morgan had given her. I looked for the papers with the address of that "place" written on it. Gone. I had to stay calm and think. We walked quickly to the lab. The door was locked. I fished for the key in the flowerpot. I unlocked the door. I didn't know what I was looking for but I knew that I would find it here. There was a note taped to the door of Dr. Morgan's office. I opened it and reluctantly I read it.

"Dear Dr. Morgan,

I have gone to Haleyville to take care of something that should make you very happy. Yours truly, Cat"

"Let's go," I said to Lola as I grabbed her by the arm. We ran down the stairs, into the street, and all the way to the bus station. Thank God, it was empty. I asked the man at the ticket counter, "when was the next bus to Haleyville", and I prayed that we were not too late. Lola and I could barely catch our breath as we talked with the man. He told us" that it would be twelve dollars for two roundtrip tickets." I had my salary from my job at the bookkeeping office. I had picked up my pay envelope that morning before meeting Lola. I handed the man the twenty-dollar bill. He gave me two tickets and my change. "When is the next bus? I asked him anxiously. "Be about ten minutes," he said. "Catch it right over there." He smiled and waved us in that direction. The bus pulled in on time, but it took the people about twenty minutes to clean the bus, gas it up, and get loaded for the trip. Lola and I didn't talk for the whole forty-minute trip. We just prayed that we wouldn't be too late.

The bus stopped. I walked up to the driver and asked him "if he could tell me where the address on the paper was, and if I needed a cab to get there?" He looked at the paper. He looked at me and said," Well it's that time of year. It's getting close to graduation time, and you girls got to be taking care of things." I knew what he meant and my heart broke for Cathy. "Please Lord don't let us be too late. He told us to" go down about a mile and turn left through a clump of open trees. Folks will show you the way". They wait for girls that look like you," he said in a sad tone, and we got off the bus. We ran as fast as we could. We passed a gas station and what looked like a grocery store. When we got there we saw Cathy lying next to an old shack. We watched as a woman came out and threw a basin of water on her. We ran to Cathy, and picked her up. The woman ran into the shack when she saw us. We heard her lock the door. We picked Cathy up under her arms and walked and dragged her to the gas station. Thank goodness Lola had come with me. I never would have been able to manage with Cathy by myself. She was dead weight with her arms around our shoulders. We went into the ladies room of the gas station and dried Cathy off as best we could with paper towels. I looked down and blood was dripping from between Cathy's legs onto my feet. Cathy fainted in our arms.

I ran out into the front of the gas station and asked if they could call an ambulance for us. The man told us to get off of his property because he didn't want any trouble with the law. We didn't know what to do. We couldn't carry Cathy. She was too heavy. Just as I turned to walk back to the restroom where Lola and Cathy were I heard a horn honking, and saw what looked like a familiar car. It was Mark Allen's car! I would know that car anywhere. It always had shiny rims and that funny shape hanging in the window. T-Bo was riding with him. I had never been so happy to see anybody in my whole life.

When Cathy opened her eyes. I was standing beside her bed. The doctor had just left. I told him that I was her sister so he told me that someone had botched Cathy up very badly. If she had not gotten to the hospital when she did she would have died. Cathy looked at me, and her eyes filled with tears. I held her hand and we both cried together. When we finally stopped crying Cathy said, "You truly are a friend. What a wonderful friend you are."

I walked out into the waiting room of the hospital and Lola was sitting there with her eyes stretched wide, and a look of concern on her face. "Is she going to be okay?" Lola asked. "Yes", I said. She will be fine in time. She had come all this way to see me, and walked into a 'hornet's nest." But she never complained. She never asked questions. She just did whatever she could without words being spoken between us. Our minds were always in sync just as they had always been. Lola was my best friend

T-Bo and Mark had walked outside for some fresh air. "I tried to explain things to them as best as I could," Lola said with a grimace on her face that I didn't understand. What did they say?" I asked. "Well T-Bo thought that it was you that was in trouble." Lola said. "Why would he think that"? I asked in amazement. "Well, it seems that T-Bo and Ray, a guy that works at the bus station, are best friends. Ray overheard us ask for tickets to Haleyville. It seems that the only reason people buy tickets to Haleyville is for why we went there. Well, Ray told T-Bo he saw us at the station buying tickets. By the time T-Bo got to the bus station with Mark Allen we had already left. So they took out after us." Lola said with a sigh. "Well how did Mark Allen get involved?" I asked. T-Bo went after Mark Allen, because he thought that you and Mark had gotten yourselves into trouble, and he was going to take care of Mark Allen. When T-Bo got to Mark, he told him he didn't know what he was talking about. T-Bo didn't believe him. So T-Bo and Mark drove over to Haleyville to find us and get to the bottom of the story," Lola said, and T-Bo and Mark Allen walked back into the waiting room.

T-Bo walked around in the room and thought about when his own children were born. He was not a religious man but he believed in God. He had been in love with Maurva Jean for as long as he could remember. They married right out of high school. T-Bo made a good living. He had his own machine shop, and got plenty of business.

His daddy had started the business over thirty years ago, and T-Bo inherited it from him. Both his parents were long since dead and T-Bo was alone in the world except for his wife and children and her family. He spoiled Maurva Jean and his children. He loved his wife's family as if they were his own people. He had proven his loyalty to them again today. He came to the rescue of his wife's baby sister, and was ready to defend her honor at the drop of a hat. "T-Bo. T-Bo," Mark Allen called. T-Bo came back to the present with a jump. "Oh yeah man. You ready to go?" "Annie ready?" he asked. "Yes, and no to your questions. Annie is going to stay the night with Cathy, and I thought I might wait around with her just in case she needs anything. I am going to drop everybody else off at home and then come back here to be with Annie," Mark Allen said casually. " I think I might stay with Annie too." Lola volunteered. Annie had walked back into Cathy's room to check on her. The other women in the room smiled when Annie walked back in. Annie had been pleasant to them and talked to them while Cathy napped,

The group went back to the room to talk with Annie about their plans. She was walking out with the doctor. Lola looked at Annie and saw how tired and worried she looked. Her dress was dirty, her hair was mussed, and her shoe had dried blood on it." "Annie said, the doctor thought it best if we all went home and let Cathy get some rest. I hate to leave her, but he says it's really nothing we can do now but let her rest. They repaired the damage as best they could. The doctor told me that whoever did that to Cathy should be put in jail."

Mark Allen and T-Bo stopped at the bus station after they took the girls home. They sat and talked with Ray for a while. "Will you pick us up about nine o'clock in your pick-up truck, T-Bo asked" "I will, and I will bring everything else that we need," Ray told them. "Good, we will be ready." T-Bo said vehemently. Mark Allen stopped by his fraternity house and talked with his friends, he told them what had transpired that afternoon. Mark and his friends changed their clothes and waited for the truck to pick them up.

When the truck arrived in front of the fraternity house, the men were dressed and ready. T-Bo was driving and Ray was in the bed of the truck. The other men got in back with Ray. Ray explained to them what was going to happen, and how they would execute their plan. The men talked among themselves, and when they were done each man knew exactly what they had to do. All of them were familiar with Haleyville. They had been connected directly or indirectly with someone that had been victimized at the hands of the workers of evil in Haleyville. Either way, they were committed to the task at hand.

The forty-minute ride took T-Bo thirty minutes. He parked the truck facing east on the opposite side of the road. The men jumped out and scattered to their designated locations. Within fifteen minutes they were all back in the truck, except for T-Bo. Ray drove the hundred yards east and T-Bo jumped in. The men in the back of the truck could see the flames rising above the trees. Ray glanced back over his shoulder just in time to see a big billow of flames shoot towards the sky, as he pulled the truck onto route 180.

As soon as the truck got back to Tuskegee the men scattered. Ray took the truck out in back of his house hosed it down, took a bath, and changed his clothes.

T-Bo changed his clothes in his machine shop. Washed his face and hands, went inside of the house, ate the cold chicken that was left over from dinner, and went to bed.

The men in the fraternity house went to their respective rooms and put the day's events behind them. Mark Allen stood outside in the night air, smoked a cigar, and thought about Annie Harris, the girl that he wanted to marry.

Lola, and Annie slept soundly that night from sheer exhaustion, unaware of what had occurred at Haleyville an hour before. Cathy Lawson lay in her hospital bed and cried herself to sleep.

The next morning the Tuskegee Herald reported the fire at Haleyville on the front page of the paper. When Maurva went to work the office was lively with conversation about the fire. Haleyville was an open secret that no one dared to discuss. Everyone in the office had their opinion of the fire, and none of them were positive. Mr. Calloway finally told everyone to get back to work and forget Haleyville. "It is over and done with, and good riddance." he said with deep emotion.

Lola had gone to class with Annie that morning just to see what it was like to be in a college class. Her professor had briefly addresses the fire with the class, and then put the matter to rest. "There will be no further discussion of that place," he said with finality. All of the students agreed, and everyone seemed relieved to move on to the next subject.

After a week of investigation the local sheriff's department had determined that one of the underground gas lines that ran from the gas station had sprung a leak, and that's what started the fire that destroyed the back section of the shantytown. Miraculously, only three people were taken to the hospital, treated for minor burns, and released. But the whole shantytown had burned to the ground. Many of the seventy-five or so people living in the shantytown were seen walking towards route 180 with their possessions in bundles on their backs. None of them would talk with the police or the newspaper. Needless to say everyone in Tuskegee was glad to see the shantytown burned to the ground, and the people gone.

Chapter 6

CATHY LAWSON SAT up in the hospital bed and ate the lunch that the nurses had brought to her. Annie came in the room and brought Cathy some fresh clothes. "Hi Annie!" Cathy said overly cheerfully. The doctor said that I could go home tomorrow. I feel great, and I need to get my work finished so that I can graduate in the spring." Cathy said. I could see right through the fake enthusiasm. I watched Cathy closely as she fiddled with the food on the plate, and I finally spoke. "Cathy, I saw Dr. Morgan today and he asked about you". Cathy turned her face to the wall. I talked on. "He seemed really worried and asked if you needed anything. I told him that I would see you later and ask you." Cathy did not move. Finally, I saw her shoulders move up and down, and I heard great sobs come from her throat. "I touched her on her shoulders and gently pulled her towards me. "Listen Cathy; I am here for you and every thing will be okay. You are going to get well. You are going to get out of this place, graduate and go on to medical school. I will do everything I can to help you. Cathy looked up at me with big sad eyes that were drowning in tears and said. "Really?" I don't understand why you would want to help me. I was always so mean to you," Cathy said between sobs. "Well Cathy some things people just can't explain. And this is one of them. Let's just move on from here and let bygones be bygones okay "friend." Cathy hugged me tightly and said "friends forever,"

Lola tapped gently on the hospital room door. She had been waiting in the lobby for me to explain to Cathy who she was and why she was here. "Come in." Cathy said. Lola came into the room and Cathy looked suspiciously at her. "Cathy, this is my best friend, Lola Brown." "Don't worry. She helped me get you here the other day". "Hello, Lola," Cathy said. Lola smiled, and took Cathy's hands in hers and said "hello friend." The two ladies hugged each other. Cathy looked at Annie and said, "Any friend of Annie's is one that I hope will become mine also." The room filled with loud deep sobs.

When we left the hospital I deliberately guided Lola towards the trail that led to the back of the dorms and the front of the fraternity houses. This path was known as Greek Row. The kids that lived back here were all members of sororities and fraternities. I had begun to wonder what had happened to Mark Allen. I had not seen him since the day that we took Cathy to the hospital. I kept telling myself that I wasn't worried, and that he would show up sooner or later. But my heart had overruled my head today. I knew exactly where his frat house was because he had taken me past it on one of our dates. He had explained to me that the symbol hanging from the mirror in his car was his fraternity emblem. It was a black and gold shield with the letters A O A on it. I asked him what it meant. He said he would explain it to me later. He said that he was an Alpha man. Mark had caps, jackets, and neckties with that same emblem and letters on it. Whenever he met another guy with the same emblems he always said; "What's up frat," and shook hands in a funny way. I always smiled when he did that, and Mark always kissed me on my cheek when I smiled at him.

On our last date, before all of the awful things happened to Cathy; Mark had said that he loved me. I looked at him, and my heart pounded in my chest. I let Mark touch me that night in a way that no one had ever touched me before. We sat there in his car a long time and just held each other. We didn't talk, and I dared not move for fear of losing the funny feelings in my head and in my body. Finally, he drove me home, helped me put on my sweater, walked me to the door, kissed me on my forehead, and said goodnight.

Mark Allen had never been a patient man. He had always managed to get what he wanted when he wanted it. Having been raised in a fairly well-off family he had things at an early age that most guys didn't have until they had their first job. He didn't have to work, but had taken the delivery job because his friend had told him that it was an easy way to meet some older girls who worked in the bookkeeping office that were "easy." Marked liked women, and had lots of experience with them. He never had a steady girl but enjoyed the company of many of them. His nickname in the frat house was "Conqueror". In the three years he had been at Tuskegee Mark had never had a girlfriend that he hadn't had his way with.

There was something different about Annie. She was kind, beautiful, and always gave him her full attention. She always had lots of questions about everything, and he was always eager to answer them. She made him feel important. It was obvious that she had no idea of his background, and she wasn't interested in marrying him for his money. Mark didn't think Annie was interested in marrying him at all. But he had made up in his mind that he would change all of that. He had to take his time with Annie. He didn't want her to feel pressured or rushed. He had to go very slowly because Annie was gentle and very fragile, and he was not about to take a chance on losing her. Mark walked onto the porch of the frat house and lit one of the tiny little cigars that all of his friends smoked, and they had sold Mark on them, so he always had a few on him. The aroma from the smoke was sweet and pungent at the same time. It was a pleasant odor that most of the girls really liked. They had told him so when he lit one after a night of love making with them. Just as he turned to walk back into the house he thought that he saw Annie walking towards the frat house. He quickly stepped off of the porch and walked towards the two girls. "Hello" he said. Trying to sound calm and cool. "What brings you two up here?' Oh "hello." Annie said. We were on our way to the dorms and we were talking so much that I forgot where I was going. "Mark, you remember Lola don't you. Mark thought to himself, how could I forget. I just spent 6 of the most grueling hours of my life with her. "Yes, hello Lola. How are you today?" Mark asked politely." I am fine," Lola said, as she took in all of the scenery and people around her. I felt as if my heart would jump out of my chest as I looked at Mark. I finally came to myself and said that we had to get to the dorm and the lab before it got too late. "Bye Mark," I said. Lola chimed in "Yes bye Mark"

We walked up the hill and around the curve to the dorms. I got that feeling again, only this time my insides melted along with that funny feeling in the bottom of my stomach. I let out a little gasp of air. Lola looked at me, and smiled that most familiar smile that had brought us through much of our childhood highs and lows. We held hands as we climbed the hill and rounded the curve leading to the dorms. Lola giggled like she did when were little girls and had a secret.

Mark walked back into the frat house. He was greeted by the whoops and oolah lah's of his frat brothers. At any other time Mark would have smiled and taken it all in, but this time he went to his room locked the door and lay on his bed. His insides ached. He had never felt like this before.

Mark had fallen asleep in his clothes. When he woke up it was six o'clock in the morning. He showered, shaved, brushed his teeth, and rushed to class. He finished his math exam and rushed to work hoping that he would see Annie. When he got there Annie was not there and neither was her sister. He finished his shift and drove back to the frat house. He thought about riding over to the house to see Annie but he changed his mind. He went to the student center instead. Mark saw lots of friends and fraternity brothers. He sat and talked for a while and left to go home. Mark drove downtown and parked his car on the grass across from the Purple Onion. He walked into the jewelry store and looked around. It was actually a jewelry/pawn shop. Mark looked around and asked to see some rings. He took his time and examined everything closely. After all, he wanted the best for Annie Harris. He was in love with her and nothing was too good for her.

Lola and Annie finished up classes and walked home. Maurva and the children were already eating supper. T-Bo was still working. We sat down and ate with the family. Maurva sat down and ate with us. The children went to their rooms to do homework. "I talked with Mr. Calloway about the Gilbert account today." Maurva said. "It seems that the figures got crossed up in the typing division. Annie it seems to have been an error on your part. Some of your numbers got crossed up with two accounts. I know that sometimes when we type we can get our decimal points mixed up. I think that I got it smoothed over with Mr. Calloway. But here is what he wants you to do. Take the rest of this semester off. It's only a few more weeks until graduation, and summer break. So when you come back you will start full time for the summer. And take classes in the evening so that you don't fall behind." Maurva offered. What do you think about that?" Maurva asked. Oh Maurva, I am so sorry. I was careless. I have so much on my mind lately. I promise that it will never happen again. Please forgive me. I hope that Mr. Calloway doesn't think too badly of me." I said pitifully. Maurva hugged me tightly. "It's okay Annie. I got it all straightened out with Mr. Calloway. It will be fine. Here, blow your nose, and go wash your face." Maurva said, as if I were one of her children.

I stumbled to the restroom and did just as Maurva had told me to do. Lola came in with a wet towel and put it on my forehead just like she used to do when we were little. "Pookie, I want you to try and get some rest. You have so much on you right now. I came to visit you and I have been nothing but a burden to you. I want to help you as much as I can." Lola said. I cried harder than ever when Lola said that. My mind went back to when we were little girls. A flood of tears came from my eyes and I cried in Lola's arms for my brother Willie Earl, and my daddy. Lola cried for her daddy, and her stolen innocence at the hands of Big Frank.

Dr. Morgan sat in his office and counted out the ten one hundred dollar bills that he had just gotten from the bank. The teller at the Tuskegee Federal Colored Teachers Savings and Loan Association had been friendly and polite as she inquired about his use for the money. "Dr. Morgan, are you going to fund another one of your research projects next fall?" She asked pleasantly. Dr. Morgan looked awkward and uncomfortable, as he quietly said no, not this time.

Morgan took the money and placed it in the white envelope that he had in his jacket pocket. He left the bank in his blue Buick Oldsmobile with the silver hood ornament. He went home, kissed his wife, talked with his children, ate dinner, and went to bed as usual. At 2oclock that morning he drove towards the school dormitory but took a quick left onto the detour road that led to the alley in back of the dorms. The man waiting there for him knew his car, and stepped onto the edge of the road so that the driver of the car could see him. Dr. Morgan rolled down the window and handed the man two envelopes. One envelope had "Sam" printed in large letters on the front. The man put that one in his jacket pocket. The other one simply had the initials CAL printed on it. He put that one in his satchel. The man had delivered an envelope every month to the same place for over a year now, so it was no big deal. This envelope seemed different. It felt thicker than the others that he had delivered in the past. He thanked the man in the blue Oldsmobile and went quickly to make his delivery.

The dorm was dark and quiet. The man left the envelope in the green plant box outside of the dorm and went back to his job at the feed store. He had a pretty good idea who the man was but he had no idea who the money was for, other than a girl who lived in the girl's dorm on campus. It didn't matter. It wasn't his business. He went about his work stacking the shelves, and filling the seed boxes. He remembered the first time that he had seen the man. He had come into the feed store and asked for someone who could run errands for him. He was a tall handsome, well-dressed man. He looked like some of the professors from the college. He couldn't really make out his features because he had worn a hat and sunglasses. Dr. Morgan gave the man directions as to where to meet him, and what he would be doing. He said he would pay $25.00 for each delivery. Needless to say the man jumped at the opportunity. Dr.

Morgan only had one request, and that was that the man was to tell no one. That was easy because the man had no family in Tuskegee and no friends. The only people the man knew were the people at the store where he worked.

Chapter 7

L OLA SAT IN the rocking chair in Annie's room. She watched Annie work on her science project and offered to help. "No, Annie said. But thanks anyway." Annie finished with her notes, took a bath and told Lola to take her turn before the kids used all of the hot water, as they usually did on school nights. Whoever was last to take their bath got the "cold bath," and that was horrible.

"Pookie, I am scared to go back home to my husband, Jackson." Lola said and she finished getting ready for bed. "Why?" Annie asked with concern in her voice. "I don't know where to begin." Lola said in a choking voice. "Just start at the beginning." I told her. "We don't have secrets between us, remember." Lola started to speak and her voice trembled as she went on. "In the beginning Jackson was so sweet and patient with me. He tried everything he could to get me to warm up to him, but I couldn't seem to be, you know, affectionate, in that way.

I listened intently as Lola talked about her struggles with having sex with her husband. We talked on into the night about Lola's problem. "Now" Lola continued, Jackson Brown had started to drink, and someone had told Lola that they had seen him at the clubs dancing with women and kissing them." Lola had cried so bitterly that I thought that she would make herself sick.

Finally, I said "Lola, I have never been married and I don't know anything about sex, but I do know that you and Jackson Brown were in love when you got married. I know that Maurva knows a lot about marriage and sex. After all she has three kids and T-Bo seems to really love her. I want you to talk to her I know she can help you. Do you want me to ask her"? I asked. "No, Pookie, I am already embarrassed enough about everything that has happened. I don't want to be a burden to anyone." Lola said pitifully. "Lola, Annie said, Maurva would be glad to help. I will talk with her tomorrow. Now let's try to get some sleep. We have a big day ahead of us tomorrow." I yawned as I said it. I watched as Lola fell off into a fitful sleep. I murmured sleepily, Lola is my best friend.

The alarm clock squealed loudly. I jumped up from the bed, and started to get ready for class. Lola rolled over and asked what time it was. "It's late," I said as I rushed around gathering my things. "Lola I said, as I rushed around the room. I am going to talk to Maurva about what we said last night." "Okay, Lola wailed as I headed out of the room. I stopped in the kitchen long enough to fill Maurva in on the details of Lola's dilemma. Then I dashed off to class.

Lola got dressed and walked slowly into the kitchen. Maurva was sitting at the table drinking a cup of coffee. She beckoned for Lola to come in. The two women sat at the kitchen table and Lola told her story to Maurva from the time she was five until her arrival in Tuskegee.

Maurva poured their third cup of coffee, and began to speak. "Lola, I understand your problem but I don't know how to fix it. "Maurva said sadly. "I do know a few people over at the college that I could talk to that might be able to help us. "Give me a day or two and I should have something figured out." Maurva said promisingly. "Now you go on and meet with Annie, before she gets worried." Maurva said." The two women hugged and Lola went on to the college to meet Annie, and Maurva went to her job at the bookkeeping office.

Annie waited for Lola at the hospital as they had planned. When they went in to get Cathy the nurse said that Cathy had left early that morning. She had checked herself out and took a cab somewhere. The nurse did not know where.

The two girls left the hospital and rushed frantically towards the dorms. When they got to Cathy's room they found her lying across the bed exhausted. The room was in disarray. Clothes were hanging out of drawers, toiletries were strewn across the bathroom, and everything was a mess. We finally got Cathy up and alert. "Cathy why did you leave without us. I told you that we were coming after class. You have got to slow down. Remember we are here for you." Annie said sternly. "I don't know what I was thinking."

Cathy said softly. "Well let's get you to bed, and get some food in you." Lola said. ' The girls fixed some food using what Cathy had in her dorm room. They all ate and fell asleep from sheer exhaustion because of what they had all been through in the last few weeks.

The girls were awakened by a loud knock on the door. Annie woke up and asked, "Who is it?" The voice on the other side answered back, "Mark Allen." Annie smoothed out her dress, and her hair and stepped outside of the dorm room and closed the door. Mark Allen looked at Annie and kissed her like she was the thirsty water he needed for his parched soul.

When Annie finally came back into the room the other two girls looked at her, at each other, and then broke out into peals of laughter. Annie was in such a daze she barely heard their laughter. She sat down on the bed next to Cathy with the widest grin and dreamiest eyes that neither one of the other girls had ever seen.

Graduation was coming in two weeks. Cathy still had lots of packing to do. She had been accepted into Howard with a full scholarship. She was going to spend the summer with her family in Cleveland before going on to Howard. She was happy these days and with the help of Annie and Lola she had learned to trust people and accept what had happened to her without complaint.

She was taking some things down from the walls when someone knocked at the door. She was sure that it was Annie and Lola, so she rushed to open the door. "It's about time you" she stopped in her tracks. It was Dr. Morgan. Cathy tried to slam the door shut, but he was too strong, and she was still as weak as a kitten and tired easily because she had lost so much blood.

Dr. Morgan pushed his way into the room. Cathy backed up against the wall and yelled for him to get out. He tried to reason with her. She was in no mood to listen and she started to throw anything that she could get her hands on at him. He finally gave up and dropped the envelope he was holding in his hand on the table and left the room. Cathy slumped to the floor and cried. When Annie came to check on her late that evening she saw a pitiful sight.

Lola had stayed home with Maurva. Maurva had a list of names for her to look over, and plenty of people that she thought might be able to help her. Some of the people on the list were professors at the college and they wanted to go over those names with Annie before they chose anyone for Lola to meet. The two ladies had become good friends and spent a lot of time talking and sharing thoughts about love and marriage. Sometimes Annie would join in and the three of them had learned so much from each other. The circle of friends was growing larger.

Annie finally came home. She had Cathy with her. Annie was afraid to leave Cathy alone anymore. She wanted her to be around people until she got stronger. Graduation was coming quickly and Annie wanted Cathy to be ready. Cathy' family was coming, and for the first time since Annie had known Cathy she had seen her smile. The three ladies went to Annie's room. After Maurva fed T-Bo and the children, and got them all settled in for the night she joined the others in Annie's room. They each shared what they knew about love, mistakes, and marriage. Annie took it all in because it was a big new frontier for her.

Maurva had spent the next two days with Lola narrowing the list of names. Annie had made suggestions as to who she thought would not be good choices. Maurva and Lola had appointments with three people. Lola had met Dr. Francine Mitchell. She was chairman of the psychology department and had often written articles about family and marriage for a new magazine just for black people called the African Gazette.

Lola had spoken with her several times, and the two ladies had really hit it off. Lola told the circle of friends that Dr. Mitchell was very familiar with her problem and offered some good advice, which she shared with us enthusiastically. Dr. Mitchell told Lola that she would have to meet with Jackson for two sessions and then meet with the both of them after that. Lola was able to pay for her sessions because of Jackson's GI bill benefits for soldiers.

The whole family drove over one Saturday afternoon to Montgomery to a big park. The park had swings, a pool, and barbeque grills. It was a park for colored people. We all had lots of fun. Cathy played dodge ball with all of the family. We were all exhausted, and everyone slept all the way home.

Lola finally got the courage to write a letter to Jackson and explain to him everything that was happening in Tuskegee. She told him about her therapy and how she wanted him to come so that he could join her in the sessions. She shared the news wit Dr. Mitchell.

We all went to church Sunday morning. It was packed with people. It was a beautiful Easter Sunday and everyone was in a festive mood. The preacher spoke about the resurrection of Jesus. My mind went back to the Easter Sunday's spent in the Live Oak Baptist church back home. The people in this church were very different from those back home. But the preaching of this minister and that of Rev. Tremble was about the same. They both reminded us that Jesus was our friend, and that he would be closer than a brother. Cathy squeezed my hand tightly when she heard that part. We all sat there and tried to concentrate on the service while we stared into the back of Dr. Morgan's head as he sat with his family. Life can be funny.

When we drove up to the house we saw a car parked out front by the curb. There was a man sitting on the porch. The man looked familiar even though I couldn't figure out who he was I knew that he was someone we knew. Lola jumped out of the car before T-Bo could come to a complete stop. She ran towards the man and they met half way. It was Jackson Brown, Lola's husband. They fell into each other's arms. They hugged and kissed for what seemed like ten minutes. Maurva escorted the children into the house and closed the door. Cathy and I went inside and helped get lunch ready.

Mark came by and we disappeared into the back yard pretending to hide eggs in the grass for the kids. Mark pulled me into the side yard near Maurva's garden. He kissed me so passionately that I could barely catch my breath.

The next few weeks flew by. Graduation was in two days. Cathy was so excited. Her family had driven down from Cleveland in a van that they had borrowed from her dad's company. They had gotten a room at the Beeline Motel.

Cathy Lawson had all of her things packed and stored in T-Bo's shed out back. She had arranged to have her belongings shipped to Howard University over the summer. We had encouraged her to use the money that Dr. Morgan had given her to pay for the shipping. Even though she had a full scholarship to Howard, she would have other living expenses. She finally gave in and set up an account at the bank and deposited the two thousand dollars in an account with the three of us as co owners on the account.

Graduation day finally came. The auditorium was filled with well wishers, family, and friends. Cathy looked beautiful. She had lost weight as a result of her ordeal, and she looked happier than I had seen her since we first met. Cathy had found two more students that were going to Howard in the fall. They had agreed to meet up when they got there. One of the friends was a guy that had really become friendly with Cathy. They had gone to a movie together, and shared a few hamburgers at the Purple Onion. It was great for Cathy's self-esteem. Things seemed to be going well with them.

After the graduation we had a big barbeque in the backyard for Cathy, her family, and her new friends. It was a great day for all.

Cathy's family left early Monday morning. They stopped by our house to thank us again. They needed to get started so that Cathy's mom and dad could get back to work. We all hugged Cathy and made her promise to stay in touch. She promised that she would. Remember, the circle of friends we said as she drove away with her family.

Lola and Jackson had disappeared shortly after we said good-bye to Cathy Lawson. They finally showed up a few minutes before their appointment with Dr. Mitchell. Lola announced that she didn't think that they would need Dr. Mitchell's services, but that they would go anyway and talk with her just in case something else came up. "Pookie, I think the late night talks with the circle of friends really helped me. I love you so much." We hugged like the friends we had become since childhood. Lola and Jackson left that afternoon as soon as their appointment with Dr. Mitchell was over.

Mark came over that evening and we discussed our plans for the future. Our first trip would be home to Georgia to meet mama and rest of the friends and family. I was happy that we were going to take care of that first. Mama and Sammy and Aunt Chauncey would be easy. Mark would love them, and they would love him. It was his family that terrified me. From what Mark had told me it might be quite a challenge. With Mark Allen by my side I felt as though I could face anything, because he was now a part of my circle of friends.

PART III

Chapter 1

I T WAS A hot day in May. It actually felt more like July than May. The grass was a deep green. Flowers were blooming everywhere, and the sun was a big bright yellow ball in the big blue morning sky. Maurva and her oldest daughter were hanging out the wash. The baby girl was playing under the sheets, just as I had done as a child. I sauntered down to the mailbox to collect the mail. I was hoping for a letter from mama. I had written her about our upcoming visit home.

Beautiful pink flower vines surrounded the mailbox pole. The box was warm to the touch. It was half open because the latch was broken. T-Bo had been promising to fix it, but he hadn't gotten around to it yet. I opened the box and put my hand inside. A swarm of bees came charging out. I screamed as they attacked my hand. Maurva, T-Bo, and the children all came running. I was running around and the bees followed me wherever I went. Maurva finally grabbed me and threw the wet sheet she was holding in her hands over me and led me to the house. The children swatted at the bees as we all ran into the house for cover.

Maurva cleaned my stings with warm soapy water and put turpentine on the red burning places. The spots where the bees had stung me had swollen quickly. "Hold still Annie" Maurva said. I jerked back every time she tried to pull the stingers out. T-Bo came running in the house. "What happened?" I could hear the yelling all the way down to the shop. " Some of the men who worked with T-Bo had come with him to see what had happened. "She is just fine Maurva said. Just some bee stings, that's all. I fixed them already. She'll be fine in a little while," Maurva cooed in Annie's face, just as she did with her children." "Well you better watch her close in case she starts to get sick." T-Bo said. " Well it will be alright. You better get on back to work. I'll send one of the children for you if I need you. Go on now." Maurva smiled as she spoke to her husband. T-Bo went on reluctantly. He was always concerned about his family, and wanted the best for them.

In all of the confusion Annie had dropped the mail. Maurva sent Lil Bo, her little boy to get it. There were several letters for Annie, and lots of bills for her. There was a letter from mama for both of them, a letter from Cathy, and one from Lola. Annie was still waiting to hear from the scholarship Dr. Morgan had promised her back in November.

Maurva opened the letter from mama. It was the usual about the folks in Madison County. Live Oak Baptist church was getting a new wing added onto the church.

They now had a new piano, and had placed the other one in the Sunday school department. Aunt Chauncey had signed up the whole county for the NAACP. All was well, and they were all looking forward to Annie coming home with Mark. Maurva took the letter in the long white envelope from among the others, and put it inside her apron pocket. She would deal with that later. She put the other mail on the kitchen table for Annie and T-Bo to read.

Annie went to lie down. She was still hurting from the bee stings. As soon as her head hit the pillow someone knocked at the front door. It was Mark Allen. T-Bo and some of his workers had seen Mark in town when they went to pick up supplies, and told him what had happened. Maurva let him in the house. He asked to see Annie. He walked back to the bedroom behind Maurva. Maurva tapped on the door. "Annie, you decent?" Somebody to see you." Annie said in a tiny pitiful voice, "just a minute." Mark Allen cringed when he heard her voice. He could not bear the thought of Annie being hurt.

Annie got up, straightened her hair, and her dress, then she opened the door. When she saw Mark the floodgates opened. She fell into his arms and cried. Maurva looked at them both and shook her head. She remembered how it had been with her and T-Bo in the beginning of their courtship. Thomas Bradford had been a wonderful husband who reminded her constantly, with his kindness, and sweet attention that he loved her. She hoped that Annie would be just as happy with Mark as she was with T-Bo.

Mark and Annie walked to the front of the house arm in arm. She offered him a chair. Mark stood there in the middle of the kitchen with a look of deep concern on his face. "Baby are you sure you are all right?" he asked. "I am fine now that you are here," Mark grabbed Annie by the hand and she let out a yell that could be heard in Madison County. Mark nearly fainted. " Oh baby I'm sorry. I forgot that was the hand that was stung. Oh baby please forgive me. Please, Please." Mark begged earnestly. Annie sat down in the chair and they all laughed hysterically. Needless to say T-Bo came running up to the back door. He ran in and they all laughed harder. T-Bo didn't get it. Maurva told him about it later that night when they were in bed.

Maurva had been holding the letter that came in the mail today close to her bosom all day long. She dared not share it with anyone until she had spoken with T-Bo about it. The doctor had confirmed two weeks ago that she was pregnant again. The house was getting smaller by the minute. Maurva had made the decision to go to the bank about a loan to add another room onto the house and a bathroom. She knew that Annie had a few more years in school. She didn't know Annie had gotten a full scholarship that had included room and board. Maurva had not paid real close attention that day when Annie came to the bookkeeping office and told her about the scholarship. It didn't really matter whether the bank had approved the loan or not now because they would make do somehow. Maurva laid the letter on the nightstand and went to sleep. T-Bo snored softly beside her in the iron bed that had been her grandmothers.

Chapter 2

ANNIE HAD PACKED her bags two days before she and Mark were scheduled to leave. She was nervous and anxious about the trip home. She had changed her dressed three times, and fixed her hair five different ways. Finally Mark arrived in his beautiful black car with the gold rims. They rode in silence for thirty minutes before speaking. " I got a letter from a sorority the other day. They have invited me to a "Rush". She said the word as if it left an aftertaste in her mouth. "Which one was it? He asked suspiciously. Annie said the words distinctly, pronouncing each one separately. "Delta Sigma Theta."

Mark brought the car to a screeching halt. He snatched the letter from her hand, read it, and crumpled it in his hands. "You will not go." He said with an angry tone. "Mark what is wrong with you? I have met some of the girls in that sorority. They have been nice to me." Annie wailed. Her voice sounded like a wounded child. "I said don't go, and I mean it." Mark yelled. "What is wrong Mark? I really don't understand." Annie moaned.

Mark got out of the car. He went around to the passenger side, opened the door and practically lifted Annie out of the car. They walked over to the dirt yard. "Listen Annie, there are so many things that you don't know about yet. When we get back to campus I will explain it to you. But for right now trust me okay." "Okay." Annie sobbed and her eyes filled with tears.

Mark could not bear to see Annie cry. He held her tightly and kissed her passionately. He could barely wait for the wedding. There were times when he felt like his insides would explode. He knew plenty of girls that could satisfy his urges, but he preferred to wait for Annie, even if it killed him. Annie climbed back into the car and Mark lit a little cigar. The aroma drifted back to the car. Anne loved the smell of the little cigars. She relaxed and enjoyed the sweet aroma.

Mark finally climbed back into the car. "Listen," he said. "Let's forget about what happened and enjoy our trip okay sweet baby." "Okay." Annie agreed. They drove the next hundred miles in silence.

The sun was beginning to set and the air was turning chilly. Annie slid over towards Mark and he welcomed her with a warm embrace. He put his arm around her shoulders and squeezed her tightly. Annie whimpered and adjusted herself in the crook of his arm. She was trying hard to fight off sleep but her eyelids were getting heavy. Annie knew that she had to stay awake because Mark didn't know the way to the house after the turn off the highway. Mark turned the radio on and he sang along with the music of Dinah Washington. Her sweet voice flowed from the radio: "_What a Good Way to Mess Around and Fall in Love_." Mark's voice reminded Annie of Lola's daddy's voice when he sang in the church choir back home, and made all the ladies get the holy ghost. Annie smiled at the thought. "What you smiling about Annie," Mark cooed in her ear. "Oh nothing." Annie said as the car moved smoothly along the road.

On Monday morning about 4 am Annie and Mark pulled onto the road that led to the house on Merritt Street. The lights were on in the house. Annie could smell the coffee as she walked up on the porch. She opened the screen door and before she could knock on the door it flung open and mama and Auntie Chauncey were out on the porch hugging and kissing her. "Lord child, let mama look at her baby. Oh my, Chauncey don't she look good? Mama said. "Yes, yes," Auntie Chauncey chimed in. "Come on in here." Mama said. "Oh mama, I want you and Auntie to meet Mark." I said. "Mark, this is mama and Auntie Chauncey." "It's very nice to know you ladies. I see where Annie gets her good looks." Mark said in his most charming voice. "Well you just come on in here and rest yourself." Mama said as she smiled and pulled Mark and the bags into the front room.

Within fifteen minutes Mama and Auntie had prepared hotcakes, eggs, bacon, sausages, grits, ham, biscuits, and gravy. We all sat down to eat. The food was delicious. Maurva was a good cook but there was nothing like mamas cooking. Mama and Auntie cleaned up the kitchen, and Mark went to the back porch for some fresh air and a smoke.

Mama had made up Willie Earl and Sammy's old room for Mark. I was going to sleep in my old room. She and Auntie would share the big bed that mama and daddy had shared for all those years, until everything went wrong.

We were both tired from the trip, and mama and auntie were tired from waiting up all night for us to get there. I walked back to Sammy's room and asked Mark if everything was okay. "Well, you didn't tell me how nice your mama and auntie are." I was really looking to meet Broom and Broom Hilda," he laughed. " Mark", I said in fake indignation. How could you think that about my sweet mama and auntie"? I chased him around the room. Mark turned around and I ran right into his arms. He kissed me, and I broke away reminding him where we were. "If you don't come here and kiss me again I will tickle you until you scream, and they will really come running," he said with sparkling mischief in his beautiful brown eyes. "No! Please Mark, don't." He came towards me and I stopped. He kissed me gently at first, then deeper and more passionately. I pulled away. "We have to stop before we get into trouble," I pleaded. "Okay, I promise to stop, I am sorry." Mark said with mock humility. I tried to walk calmly back into the front room. Mama and auntie looked at me with little smiles on the corners of their mouths. I went to bed wondering what they were thinking.

I had a fitful sleep. I dreamed about Willie Earl, and the horrible way that he was murdered. I could see Big Frank as he tried to rape me, and how he did rape Lola. I could see

Lola's daddy fall to the ground that day after court when the judge set him and daddy free. I finally woke up to a quiet house.

I wandered out into the living room remembering to put on my robe in case Mark was up and about. I found a note on the kitchen table. It said that mama, auntie, and Mark had gone into town to shop. I wandered around the house. I touched each piece of furniture. Each piece brought back special memories of times gone by.

Mama had added a bathroom with a shower and tub to the house while I was gone. It was great to step in and get cleaned up without a big fuss. I thought that I would wash my hair while they were gone. I stepped out of the shower to look for some shampoo when I heard the front screen door slam. "Oh goodness" I said. "They got back sooner than I thought." I dried myself off and quickly slipped into my underwear. "Annie, Annie", mama called from the front room. "Yes ma'am. I'm back here mama." I called back to her. I got dress quickly, and combed my hair.

Mama came into the bedroom, took off her hat, and her dress. She slipped into her housedress while she talked on and on about Mark, and the trip to town. "That Mark is such a gentleman." She said. "Do you know that he would not let me pay for one thing?' He paid for the groceries, and Chauncey's medicine. "I tell you he is something special, yes something special." She said as she buttoned her dress. "Well, I am going to get dinner started. Chauncey stopped at the Johnson's house. Mrs. Johnson has the miseries, and she is down in her back. Come on and help me with dinner."

Mama said. "Okay mama. I am almost finished dressing. Let me get my shoes. " I yelled from under the bed where I had stuffed the suitcases,"

When I came out mama and Mark were shelling peas. Mark looked funny with the apron tied high across his broad chest. " He is catching on quick." Mama said. Mark smiled broadly at the compliment. I eased over to the other side of the table and turned my back. I was trying my best not to laugh. Mark looked cute and funny at the same time with mama's apron tied around his chest. He was seriously working at shelling the peas. His forehead was filled with creases as he focused intently on getting the peas shelled and into the pan without spilling any on the floor. I couldn't hold it any longer. I burst into laughter. Mark and mama looked at me as if I had two heads. "What's so funny?' they both asked at the same time, with serious expressions on their faces." "Nothing." I said and ran back into the bedroom.

I fell on the bed with my face buried in the pillow to stifle my laughter. I began to think about all of the happy times we had enjoyed in this house when I was growing up. I got up and walked into the backyard. I went into the smokehouse. I saw Willie Earl's red wagon. I walked over to the wagon and pulled the handle. I sat down beside the wagon and I started crying. I don't know why I was crying. All at once I felt so many emotions. I was happy for my friendship with Mark. At the same time, I was sad for my daddy, and my dead brother Willie Earl. I was an emotional wreck.

Mark came from the house calling me. "Annie, Annie where are you?' I wiped my face with the back of my hand, smoothed my hair, and clothes, and ran towards Mark's voice. "Coming," I said as happily as I could manage. "What's up?" Mark asked suspiciously. "Are you ok?' he asked anxiously. "I am fine Mark." I said as I turned my head and tears rolled down my cheeks and onto my dress. Mark knew everything about my family. I had shared with him about daddy's affair, the sack, the letters, Lola, Big Frank, and my brothers Sammy and Willie Earl's lives in the house on Merritt Street. I didn't keep anything from Mark, because I trusted and loved him very much. I had come to realize that I loved Mark and cherished his friendship as I cherished Lola's. I had settled it in my heart the first day that we walked into the house Merritt Street.

Mark held me close and told me everything was going to be okay. We started to walk out into the pasture. The grass was prickly against my legs. When we got to the spot where Lola and I had buried the sack I stopped and looked at Mark. He looked at me and said, "We are going to settle this right now baby. Wait here. I will be right back."

Mark came back with a shovel, some old rags, and a flashlight he had found in the smoke house. " Listen to me" Mark said. "We are going to dig up this sack and settle this issue once and for all." Mark spread the rags out on the ground. He told me to sit down and think about the exact location of the sack. I didn't have to think for very long because the spot was free of grass. and debris. It was as if the spot was waiting for us to come to it and settle the issue once and for all. We found the spot. Mark started digging. I sat on the rags that Mark had spread on the ground and held the flashlight for him to see the spot and locate the sack.

It was dark when we walked back to the house with the sack between us. I somehow felt that this was something Willie Earl wanted us to do, and I was no longer betraying his trust. The backdoor slammed as we walked into the house with the sack.

Mama and Chauncey were busy fixing the table for dinner. "Where ya'll been. Go wash up before everything gets cold. Mark, I have everything laid out for you in the spare room." Mama said. Mama had started to call Willie and Sammy's old room the spare room. Mark went to the spare room, and I went to my room. We were both back at the table in five minutes. We were all starving and ate the delicious food hungrily. We all pitched in and cleaned up the kitchen. We went to the porch for some air.

We sat on the front porch. The rain came down with a vengeance. We were sitting far enough back from the edge of the porch to stay dry. Mark got in the hammock. Mama, Auntie, and I sat in the swing. Mama fanned with one of the old Rooker funeral home fans. I thought about how Willie Earl would get the fans out the trashcans that the white folks had thrown away. He would fix the broken handles. Then he would take them to the church for the colored folks to use on Sunday mornings to fan themselves because the church was so hot. Mama had written to me that the church had raised enough money to buy two window air conditioners. They had put one of them in the sanctuary, and the other one in the new fellowship hall. The church finally had air conditioning, which was one luxury mama still didn't have.

Mama got up and announced that we should all turn in because it was obvious that Mark was tired because of the way he was snoring in the hammock. I tapped Mark on the shoulder. He said he would be right in. I went to bed. I looked out of my window and I didn't see Mark in the hammock. The car was gone. I didn't know what to think. Maybe he had gone into town for some cigarettes. I finally dozed off to sleep.

I felt someone shaking me. I sat up startled by the shake. It was Mama. "Where is Mark honey?' she asked. "I don't know I said sleepily. I saw last night in the hammock when we went to bed." Well he probably went to the store for some of those funny little cigars that smell so fine, mama said. " Mama, I think I am going to wash my hair." Will you press it for me?"

I was sitting on the same stool that I had sat on as a child when mama did my hair. Mama pressed my hair and the grease made it shine. We talked about my fights with my head rag at night. Mama said that she knew about me taking the rag off every night and having a nappy head in the mornings was my punishment. So she never said a word about it.

Just as mama was finishing my hair we heard a car. I ran to the window just as Mark and another man that I couldn't quite make out who he was until he got closer. It was Mr. Curtis. He and Mark were carrying a big box. They came to the door, and mama rushed to push back the screen. They came in and sat the box down in the middle of the floor. "Well hello there Annie," Mr. Curtis said, as he hugged my neck. How you doing?' Fine Mr. Curtis, just fine." I said. "I met Mr. Curtis when I was coming out of the hardware store. He offered to help me with my package. Mark said as he wiped his forehead with the back of his hand. I introduced myself to him, told him where I was staying, and he volunteered to help me with this little project." Mark said as he pointed to the box on the floor. Mark told me to take mama into town shopping. He said for us to come back in three hours. It was a good thing that Auntie Chauncey could drive because it was too hot to walk.

We took Mark's car and drove into town. We stopped in at Neumans, and the Five and Dime. Mama bought some thread, and other little knick-knacks. Auntie Chauncey bought some snuff. The time went quickly. The clock on the top of the courthouse chimed four times. It was 4 o'clock. Time to go home. We got into Mark's car and Auntie Chauncey drove us to the house on Merritt Street.

The house was cool and dark. The curtains were drawn and mama opened the door and we all walked in slowly not knowing what to think. We walked into the front room. It was so cool and dark. We went into the kitchen. Mark and Mr. Curtis were drinking beer. They both got up when they saw us. "Well? Mark said with a big grin on his face. How do you like it?" Mama and me and Auntie looked at each other. We didn't know what he was talking about. "Didn't you notice how cool it was when you came in? He asked.

"Yes, I said, but" Mark took me by the hand and motioned for Auntie and mama to follow.

We stood there in the front room and felt the cool air blowing all around us. Oh my Lord! Mama said. "This boy done went and bought us a air conditioner." Mark, I stammered. You bought this for us? Oh Mark this is too much." "Nothing is too much for my wife to be, and my soon to be new family." Oh Mark, I cried, and fell into his arms. Mama, Auntie, and Mr. Curtis all cried with me. Mark walked over to mama and took both of her hands in his and asked; "Mama, I mean Mrs. Harris, may I please have your daughter for my wife." Mama finally found her voice. "Yes baby." she said. Then Mark came back to me, got down on his knees and asked me to be his wife. "Yes" I said after I stopped sobbing and caught my breath. " I will be your wife." Needless to say the house was filled with tears of joy for the good news that had come to Merritt Street. While we all celebrated, Mr. Curtis eased quietly out of the front door.

Chapter 3

MARK PACKED THE last of our things into the car. Mama, Mark, and I sat down and planned a lot for our life before we left for Tuskegee. Mark had taken the sack and put it in a deep dark place in the trunk of his car. He said we would deal with it when we came back for the wedding. That was fine with me. He gave mama and auntie some last minute instructions on how to work their new air-conditioner. Mama had fixed us a lunch of fried chicken and potato salad. Auntie Chauncey had made hot buttered rolls, and banana cake for dessert.

We got into the car and headed back to Tuskegee We drove all the way without stopping to use the restroom. We got to Maurva and T-Bo's late in the afternoon. Mark brought my things into the house and put them in the living room. He spoke to everyone, pecked me on the cheek, and headed out of the door.

Maurva, T-Bo and the whole family bombarded me with questions about everybody at home. I told them about the air conditioner, and the rainy night on the porch. Maurva was so excited about the trip and the air conditioner

When I got to the bookkeeping office everyone was already working hard. I went to my desk and uncovered my typewriter. There was a letter addressed to me from another sorority.

Dear Miss Harris,

Please join us for an afternoon tea, Saturday next 5p.m. Gamma Gamma Hall, Tuskegee University.

Regrets, 559-3614

Sincerely, Helen Finely

Helen Finley, Grammaticus, Alpha Kappa Alpha, Sorority

Oh no, not another one. This one may upset Mark also. I thought to myself. Mark had become very upset about the first letter from the girls that wore the red and white outfits on the campus. They had been so nice to me. They always smiled and waved hello to me when I walked across campus. The girls that sent me this letter never said hello to me. They had been rude to me in the library. When I waited for Mark in the Purple Onion one night, some of them were sitting across from me. I thought that they were making fun of me but I wasn't really sure. When Mark walked in they smiled and called him by name. They pretended to be nice to me when he was around. They called him "frat" and exchanged friendly greetings with him.

I hid the letter in my desk and started working on the pile of files on my desk. Mark came in after lunch. "Hey baby" what's new? Mark asked sweetly. He was looking around on my desk. Finally he asked; "Did you get any interesting mail today?" I knew at that moment he knew. He had probably delivered it himself that morning before I got to the bookkeeping office. "No, not really, I said. I was not a very good liar, especially to Mark. It was as if we knew each other's souls. "Oh" he said as his eyes continued to canvas my desk. I stared at my typewriter and I started to cry. "Yes, I mean no. I mean I got another one of those letters today. Only from a different group of girls, I sobbed. "Oh Mark, I don't know what to do." First of all calm down it's okay". I handed Mark the letter from my desk. "I don't know what to do? " I said between sobs. "Are you upset? I sobbed. "Please don't be upset." I cried. "It's okay. I am not upset." Mark said as he read the letter" "This is great! Baby this is where you want to be. "It is? I asked in amazement. "Yes, baby if you do this we will be a team. You will be my sorority sister. I will be your fraternity brother." Mark said with a big wide grin that showed his perfectly beautiful smile. Mark grabbed me and twirled me around the room. "We can make this happen." He said. Mark practically ran out of the book keeping office. He tipped over a few boxes as he left. Mr. Calloway looked at Mark, then at me and frowned.

The next few weeks were hectic. I had so much to do and so much to learn. I was pledging. I was on line. I had a new name that my soon to be sisters gave me. It was "Lil Weenie." I was beginning to enjoy being a part of things. I was beginning to understand all of the symbols, and things that I had seen Mark wear, and display in his car, and on his clothing.

The big day finally came. It was beautiful. I was now officially an AKA. It opened a whole new world for me. I went to meetings, parties, and dances. I bought paraphernalia, pink sweaters, green dresses with little pink flowers. It was all so grand.

Mama and Auntie Chauncey came to visit and we started planning the wedding. Maurva told us that she had a surprise for us. She told us that she was pregnant. It was an incredible time of excitement. Maurva told us that she and T-Bo wanted to help with the wedding. They had come into a little money and they wanted to help. Mama cried. I cried. Auntie Chauncey cried. We all hugged each other and sat quietly thinking of our good fortune.

T-Bo let himself in the back door. He didn't want to wake up the house. It was late and he had spent the evening working on parts in his shop. He was tired and exhausted. He tiptoed quietly into the bedroom. Maurva was in the bathroom. He thought that she was having sickness spells again. He could hear her through the door. "Baby you okay," he asked through the door. She didn't answer. He called her again. T-Bo went in the bathroom and found Maurva on the floor. "Hey baby, you okay? T-Bo asked. "Yes" she said. "I just had a bad spell this time. I can tell that this baby is going to be strong willed with a mind of his own." Maurva moaned. Maurva and T-Bo made love right there on the bathroom floor that night. T-Bo was very gentle and careful.

He dared not hurt Maurva or the baby he thought as they held each other tightly. They finally went to bed and slept peacefully until morning. Maurva stirred when she thought she smelled bacon.

Bea Harris was not one to lie around. She and Auntie had been up since 5am. They had made breakfast for the whole family. Ray and Mark had come over to eat with the family. We finished breakfast and left for church.

That afternoon Mama, Maurva, Auntie Chauncey, and I worked out many of the details for the wedding. We picked the colors, the people, called Rev. Tremble to confirm the date and the church, and talked with Mark about the rehearsal dinner and the engagement.

Mark spoke with his parents about his engagement to Annie. They were excited about the engagement, and all of the activities that were planned for the couple. Mark's mother told him of her plan to have an engagement party for them. The engagement party would be a good time for the families to meet, and for them to get to know Annie.

"Mark I hope that your parents approve of me." Annie said quietly. "Oh Annie baby you are too wonderful for anybody not to like you. My mother can be a bit of a snob, but she is okay once you get to know her. My dad is great. You will really love him." Mark said lightly. "I hope that they will like my family" Annie said as she held tightly onto Mark's arm. "Don't worry so much, Lil Weenie" Marked teased. Mark left Annie's house and drove to the store where he had ordered Annie's ring. The man had said that it would be ready in about a month. That had given Mark enough time to get the money that he would need to buy the ring.

Mark and Annie planned their trip to Mississippi. It was a longer trip to Mississippi from Tuskegee than the one to Madison County from Tuskegee. They planned to have the engagement party while they were there. Mark's mom asked for a list from Annie of friends and family that she wanted to invite so that she could send out invitations. Annie got her list together. She sat at her desk and wrote the names of the people that she wanted to invite. She thought of the friends she had met at Tuskegee, friends from home, and of course her sorority sisters. The list was long, but Annie didn't want to leave anyone out. She finished her work and went home.

Mama and Auntie Chauncey were packed and ready to go to the bus station. Annie, Mark, and Maurva went with them. The bus came on time. They waved the bus out of sight and drove back to the house.

Mark and Annie sat on the porch and talked until dark. He kissed her goodnight and drove back to the frat house. Mark took the ring he had bought for Annie from his storage box and examined it closely under the light from the lamp on his desk. It was a beautiful ring with a gold band and a neat diamond in the middle. He had asked his dad for a loan so that he could get the ring. His dad had graciously given him the money and some extra just in case. His dad was a great guy who drank a little too much but he was able to hold his liquor without anyone knowing that he was drinking. Mark's mother was very different from his father. She had money and had helped his dad get started in his business and she never let him forget it. Mark's grandfather could pass for white and had been a very successful doctor in Mississippi. Mark's mother was very proud of her background and never let the people in Jacksonville forget it. She had decided to be a teacher. Truth be told, Mark's mom did not make the grades necessary for studying medicine.

Mark's sister had finished school at Tuskegee and Howard and was a doctor with her husband in Africa. Mark had written to her and told her all about his plans for marriage and about how much he loved Annie. He was very close to his sister and wanted her approval more than anyone else in the world. Rose loved Mark and they had been close since childhood. She wanted him to be happy. They had a few close calls as teenagers. She kept his secrets and he kept hers. They had vowed to never betray each other and so far they had not let each other down.

Rose and her husband Robert Lee had told Mark that they would come for the wedding but not for the engagement party. It would be too expensive to go and come in such a short period of time.

Rose Mary had been born with a birth defect. Her right leg was about a ¼ of an inch shorter than her left leg. It wasn't very noticeable. Her mother had chosen her shoes carefully. She had them made in Chicago and shipped to Mississippi. No one in Jacksonville ever knew, or so her mother thought. One day some of the children in the neighborhood were playing under the streetlight. Rose had fallen on the ground trying to kick a ball, and a boy had called her a cripple. Rose had cried. Mark could not bear to see his sister cry. He had beaten the boy and bashed his head with a rock. Mark had beaten the boy so badly that the boy almost died. This was one time that his mother's money came in handy. His grandfather had treated the boy for free. When his grandfather could do nothing further for the boy they sent him to Tupelo and Mark's parents paid for all medical treatment, bus rides, and supplies. They also paid the family $1,000 hush money. They were a very poor family with no money to hire a lawyer. They also knew that no judge black or white would go against old man Winston. John Winston was a colored man that could and did pass for white when it was beneficial to him and his family, and so could his children. That was the only reason that Mark missed being sent to prison.

When Rose was a teenager she got involved with a boy from another part of town. They had gone too far. The family had prepared to send Rose to New York to live with her aunt. Rose's mother carried on vehemently until Rose left. She told Rose that she was a disgrace to her family, and that she never wanted to see her again. Needless to say Mr. Allen drank heavily during that time and withdrew deeper into himself. Mark learned to cope with it all by helping his grandfather with his practice, Mark would talk to the patients about their sick crops, and crop rotation while his grandfather took care of their sick bodies.

While in New York Rose went riding on a roller coaster at a local amusement park. It was a beautiful Sunday afternoon. Her aunt insisted that Rose ride the roller coaster with the other children. Rose, in her delicate condition could not withstand the jerks and pulls of the roller coaster. She became ill and had to go home immediately. She lost the baby that night in the bathtub. Rose came back home a few weeks later. She was thin and frail. Her mother was happy because no one ever knew that Rose had gotten pregnant. It took Rose months to come back to her normal self. It was Mark who helped her through the painful experience. They have been extremely close every since.

The bond between Rose Mary and her mother was never mended. They barely spoke to each other. On occasion when they happen to cross paths it is always with a strained politeness that is noticeable to anyone around them.

Mark continued to study the ring. There was a knock on his door. He came back to himself. "Just a minute" he said as he placed the ring back into its safe place in the box. He opened the door and it was Champ, his fraternity brother. They were very close because they had been line brothers in the fraternity. "What's up frat?" Champ asked as they clasped hands in a fraternal handshake. "It's all good. "I brought you something." Champ said. Champ handed Mark an envelope. "Thanks man" Mark said. "No problem" Champ said, as he left the room. Mark sat down on the bed and opened the letter. It was a letter from his mother. She had planned the engagement party, had the invitations ready, and arranged lodging for everyone scheduled to attend if they needed it. She had arranged for the country club to be ready on a short notice, if necessary. She was waiting for a final date from Mark in order to confirm everything.

Mrs. Allen was considered a snob and a stuck –up bitch by all who encountered her. She was a beautiful woman. She had been queen of Mississippi Colored State College. She was medium height with light skin and long legs. She looked white, but if you looked closely you could tell that she was a Negro. Her lips were full, and her hair had a wavy pattern. Her nostrils really gave her away. They were pointed at the top but flared out at the bottom. Mrs. Allen wore the best dresses, had fur stoles, and a beautiful set of diamond wedding rings that she had bought and paid for year's earlier herself.

Her father had spoiled her and allowed her to have anything his money could buy. Her mother had died in childbirth, and her father tried to compensate for it by giving her things. Sweetie Bell Winston Allen was respected in her community but not well liked.

The family home was brick. Her father and grandfather had built it. Mrs. Allen had added to the house, and had it redone several times. It was now red brick with white shingles, and a white door. The inside was immaculate. The furniture was covered in heavy plastic and the rugs were shag and trimmed in pink and green. There were pictures of family members, sorority events, and pictures of Mark and Rose when they were babies. There was a single picture of Mrs. Allen in her wedding dress. There were no pictures of Mark's father anywhere in the house.

Chapter 4

THE SUMMER FLEW by. Annie and Mark were inseparable. When they weren't working at the book keeping office they were enjoying the long summer nights on the back porch in the swing at the house Annie had called her home away from home. They could barely hold hands because Maurva's children were running around the house chasing fireflies, and playing Red light. They tried kissing once or twice but the children always caught them and threatened to tell Maurva. Mark and Annie just gave up. They would sit most of the time with the children between them in the swing. The children often fell asleep in their laps.

Annie still went to the lab and did as much as she could to stay ahead. Her new scholarship would begin in the fall. Annie often ran into Dr. Morgan at the lab. She spoke politely and went about her business. Dr. Morgan had a funny look in his eyes. It seemed as if he were asking a thousand questions without speaking a word.

Annie was working late in the lab. Dr. Morgan was in his lab office. Annie cleaned up and was hanging up her lab coat when someone knocked on the door. It was Mark. "Hey baby, I came to take you home." Mark said. Just as they were leaving Dr. Morgan came out of his office. "Hello frat" Dr. Morgan said to Mark. "What's up my brother A.C ?" Mark said to Dr. Morgan. They exchanged handshakes. "We have a new little sister, Dr. Morgan, Mark grinned as he hugged me. "I heard. I heard, Dr. Morgan said with a pleasant grin. "I am so proud of her. That is why I am going to make her my wife." Mark grinned. "So I heard." Dr. Morgan said as he gathered up his things. "Congratulations, and best wishes to you Annie, he said as he walked out of the door. "Goodnight," he called over his shoulder. He closed the door gently behind him.

Mark and I went straight home. I was tired from my long day and so was he. He walked me to the door, kissed me on the cheek and left. I went in the house, ate dinner, took a bath and went to bed.

I woke up and heard the wind whipping at the side of the house. The thunder and lightning was strong. I heard the family in the living room. I got up and Maurva came through the door. "Get your boots on, and your coat. T-Bo said we are going down into the storm cellar." Maurva said tensely. T-Bo had dug it out himself, and took great pride in keeping it stocked with supplies. We had gone down to see his latest work one Saturday afternoon. T-Bo had added some poles and sided up the walls. It looked like a regular room. We had our lanterns. The blankets were already in the cellar. Just as we stepped into the backyard everything went black. The lightning was sharp and lit up the sky. The thunder shook the ground as we went into the cellar. The wind was strong. We held on tightly to each other.

Mark and the others in the frat house huddled in the basement of the house. The storm was fierce, with strong winds and bright lightning. It raged on most of the night. We could hear it from the cellar.

When we came out of the cellar the next morning debris and trash was scattered everywhere. The roof was torn half way off of the house. Water was everywhere. The children started to cry. Maurva, T-Bo, and I started to gather up whatever we could and took it to the cellar. While we were cleaning my mind wandered to Mark. I prayed that he was safe.

We worked all day putting things in the cellar. Ray had walked to our house from across town. He said that our neighborhood was the hardest hit. Other people had minor damage but we were the only ones who had lost our roof. Ray and some of the other guys from the machine shop helped T-Bo get a tarp over the roof. They worked hard repairing other parts of the house. We all worked until we couldn't see anymore. Some of the neighbors brought us food, and ice tea. We all ate, and went to sleep on cots in the back part of the house that still had a roof.

I woke up to the sound of hammering and sawing. I sat up on the cot and ran to look out of the front door. I saw what looked like a small army hammering and sawing on the house. There were some men working on every part of the house. I saw Mark and a group of guys dressed in jeans and black and gold shirts. They were his frat brothers. They came to help clean up and repair our home. When I saw them I started crying. Mark saw me standing in the door, and came rushing towards me. "Hey baby girl. What's up?" He said with love and concern in his voice. "Nothing, I am just so proud of you and your friends." I love you Mark Allen, I said through tears. Mark kissed me passionately. I almost fell out of the door. "Uh um, excuse me. Is this where Annie lives?" T-Bo said, as he tapped Mark on the shoulder. I ducked back inside of the house embarrassed to have let Mark kiss me in public like that. I heard Mark talking and laughing with to T-Bo.

While the men continued their work on the house we all got dressed and went downtown to run errands. We went to the furniture store, the Five and Dime, the hardware store, and Bracken's Appliances. Maurva took notes and talked to all of the friendly salesmen. They all talked about deals and sales. Maurva continued on as if she didn't hear them. She checked fabrics, she rubbed her hand across chairs, and sat on long couches, soft couches, round couches, and furry couches. We went into the Five and Dime. I watched Maurva look at curtains, towels, rugs, and coffee pots, while she took notes. Finally, we stopped at Bell's Café. Maurva treated us all to Bell's Special. It was great! We had ice cream for dessert. The ice cream reminded me of ice cream on the front porch at home on Merritt Street.

We walked uptown to the Tuskegee Federal Colored Teachers Savings and Loan Association where most of the

Negroes in Tuskegee had their money, cashed their checks, and bought savings bonds for their children. You didn't have to be a teacher to bank there. When we walked in all of the people smiled at us and asked to help us. I sat on the couch with the children, and Maurva went to the window to speak with the teller. I watched as he motioned with his hand to the people at the desk on the other side of the big room. Maurva walked over to the tables and the handsome Negro man in the blue suit held out a chair for her to sit down.

Maurva finished her business and we went out in the afternoon sunshine. "Well we can get things replaced in the house and still have money to pay for your reception Annie," Maurva said joyfully. "The storm was a blessing in disguise Maurva, but I don't want to put a strain on you with the reception." I said. "Annie, if I had to work two jobs to help with your wedding I would do it. God has blessed us and now we are going to bless you. We love you little sister." We all held hands, with the children in the middle, and walked happily down the street.

We walked into the yard and we couldn't believe our eyes. The children broke free and ran up to the porch. The roof was repaired, the water was mopped up, and all of the ruined furniture was in the back of Ray's pick-up and T-Bo's pick-up trucks. Maurva was delighted. I ran to my bedroom. Thank goodness that part of the roof was left intact. I had not lost anything. There was sawdust and debris everywhere. It wouldn't take long to clean that up. I was so happy that everyone had pitched in to restore the roof. Mark and his friends had done a great job. T-Bo and his friends had worked hard for us to have a roof over our heads before nightfall.

T-Bo and Maurva sat down and discussed the money from the bank and how they would spend it. T-Bo was excited about helping Annie with the wedding, and with getting things repaired. "Annie, we are so happy to be able to help you with your wedding." T-Bo said as he walked out of the house for work. I barely had a chance to thank him before the backdoor slammed shut. Maurva and I went to work at the book keeping office and stayed so busy we didn't see each other until time to go home. Mark had delivery after delivery, and we only saw each other in passing.

I fixed dinner so that Maurva could put her feet up. We ate dinner in the back yard on the folding table. We had chicken, rice, rolls, and peach cobbler for desert. Everybody loved my cobbler. We finished dinner. The children played in the yard until dark, and then they went inside for their baths. Maurva and I sat in the swing and talked about the engagement party, the wedding and the reception.

Maurva went shopping for furniture, curtains, bedspreads, and other household items. We spent hours shopping for things that matched and coordinated with the colors that the rooms in the house had been painted. It was great fun. We grew closer as sisters as time for the baby grew nearer.

Maurva was nice and round. Her belly was dropping lower and lower everyday. The baby was due in a month. When the men were repairing the house they had added a little room adjacent to T-Bo and Maurva's room. It was a mini nursery. It was painted yellow with a green border. There were shelves against the walls, and room for a crib and changing table. It was a beautiful little place. Maurva was busy shopping and making things for the nursery. They had given her a shower at the office and everyone had been very generous. Maurva's friends in the neighborhood, and from her church had brought her many gifts for the baby.

We all went to bed early that night because we were so tired from all of the activities that had happened that week. I sat in the rocking chair and looked out of the window. It was a beautiful chilly October night. The moon was round and full. It was a deep yellow. Just as I was getting into bed T-Bo tapped on my door. "Annie we are on our way to the hospital. Do you mind staying with the kids"? T- Bo asked nervously. "Oh it's time? I asked giddily. "Yeah, we will let you know when something happens." He said as he helped Maurva to the car. They drove off into the dark night.

October 5, 1961 at 12:35 pm, a baby girl was born. She was beautiful. She had curly black hair, and big dark eyes. She was the most beautiful baby I had ever seen. Maurva looked beautiful. She had gotten all cleaned up. People were coming from church, and the neighborhood. They brought more gifts, fruit baskets, diapers and bottles. The room was full of flowers from friends and neighbors. T-Bo had given Maurva a beautiful bouquet of roses. It was a wonderful day. Leola Mary Bradford

Maurva and T-Bo brought the baby home the next week. The house was filled with people everyday. Maurva stayed in bed. I cooked and cleaned, went to classes, and the lab. It was hectic but I did it. " I think that we are ready for our first day up and out of bed." Maurva sang sweetly. The doctor had given strict orders for Maurva to stay in bed. She had lost a lot of blood during Leola's birth. They had chosen to name the baby after T-Bo's mother. The name seemed to fit the baby's personality well. She was quiet, gentle and had such a sweet demeanor. We all started to call the baby "Red" because she had just a sprinkle of red hair in the middle of her head. Everyone loved little Red. The other children treated her like she was a doll. They carried her, around in their arms, and played with her. "Little Red" was really loved.

Mark Allen was very busy. He had an overload of classes, and he was still working at the bookkeeping shop. I looked forward to our Thursday afternoon dates. We started meeting at the Student Center. Most of the things we did now were free. We had to save our money for the wedding. We took long walks. We went to the park. We went to Mark's dorm once. We almost went too far. We decided not to do that again. We found lots of ways to have fun, and spend time together.

Mark spent a lot of time teaching me how to drive. I caught on quickly. I drove myself to the license bureau. We walked into the building and went to the license bureau section. And sat in the area marked Colored. We walked to the window and the woman said her window was closed. Mark and I walked to the next window and the woman asked for my identification. I handed her my wallet with my college identification card in the front. She picked it up as if it was dirty. She wrote down my student number and pushed the wallet back to me with her pencil. She walked away and yelled over her shoulder for us to go and sit down. We sat in the lobby for two hours. We watched people in the white section go and come all morning. Finally, Mark went to the window. "Excuse me, he said to the woman who had taken my application, we have been here for two hours. Can you tell us how much longer it will be?" Mark asked politely. The woman closed the window and said, "Come back tomorrow."

We sat on the porch at the house. It was hard to wrap our minds around what had happened that day. Mark smoked one of his little cigars. The aroma always seemed to make me settle down. "Listen, tomorrow we are going back to that place and if things don't go right they will be sorry. Mark said angrily " I sat there in the green swing on the back porch, and closed my eyes, and prayed that all would go well tomorrow." Please Lord let it be alright." I said under my breath.

We left for the license bureau early the next morning. We walked up to the same window. The same woman was there. "I need to give this application for a driver's license to someone," Mark said in an authoritative manner. " I am closed," the woman said. Mark took me by the hand and we went to the next window. "I would like to give this application for a driver's license to someone. We filled it out yesterday, and when we tried to give it to someone they said the office was closed." Marks said again, in an even more authoritative tone. The woman said that the application was not valid and we would have to fill out another one. The woman threw the application to Mark and walked away. Mark picked up the application. We walked to the counter, filled it out and brought it back to the counter. The woman took the application and told us that it would be a fee of $25.00 cash to process the application. Mark took all of the money from his wallet, but it was ten dollars short. I had money in my purse. It only amounted to $7.80. I started to cry. Mark was beginning to get angry. Just as we were about to leave the office, a woman came up to us and asked us how much we needed. Mark told her that we were about $2.20 short. The woman told us to give her the money we had. Mark reluctantly gave it to her, and then she gave us two ten-dollar bills and a five-dollar bill. Mark told her we would pay her back. He asked her for her name and address but she wouldn't give it to him. Mark thanked her and told her that she was very kind and looked very familiar. She walked back to her seat. I walked over and sat down next to her while Mark took the application back to the window. "Hello, my name is Annie, Annie Harris" I said. "I am pleased to meet you Annie." The woman said. "I didn't get your name" Annie said." "Well if you must know, my name is Betty Morgan" Annie rolled the name around in her head, then she spoke" You wouldn't by chance be related to Dr. Abraham Morgan on Tuskegee campus?" she asked politely. "I am," the woman said uneasily. "Please, just keep it to yourself," she pleaded. The woman left the building quickly.

Mark walked over to me. "Did you get her name?" Mark asked. "I did. Mark she asked that we would forget about it. She only wanted to help." "That's fine Mark said with a puzzled look on his face. I went to the window, got my license and we left that awful place and hurried down the stairs to the car.

Chapter 5

MARK HAD RECEIVED his internship appointment at the Tuskegee County Agent office. He was going to be an Assistant Field Marshall. Mark had to cut his hours at the bookkeeping office. They loved Mark at the office and did not want to lose him. They allowed him to come in two afternoons a week and make all of his deliveries. It was hard juggling all of his assignments as Assistant Field Marshall and making deliveries but he was determined to manage.

T-Bo had fixed up one of the cars he had stored at his machine shop. Some of his customers would leave old cars as payment for work T-Bo did for them. T-Bo had gotten this particular car from his friend Ray who worked at the bus station. Ray had seen me, and Lola take the bus to Haleyville that awful day sometime back. He actually saved Cathy Lawson's life. Things could have been a lot worse for us if T-Bo, Mark, and Ray hadn't shown up when they did.

T-Bo had gotten the car for me and Maurva to use whenever we needed to run errands It was a big help to me to have that car. Maurva didn't like driving so she rarely used the car. Maurva said she liked taking the bus or have me drive her around. Maurva and I really enjoyed each other's company.

The weather turned cold. I started my dual studies program in Montgomery at the Negro Women's Center. Dr. Morgan had started his new program on venereal diseases in women. He appointed me chairperson of the project. I spent most of the day collecting samples from the women at the center. I had spent a lot of time collecting animal samples in the lab so I felt like I was prepared for anything.

I had come to the center early that morning. There was a young woman sitting on the steps. She was shaking, and scratching herself. Her eyes looked wild and her hair was knotted all over her head. It looked as if she never tied her hair up in a headscarf at night. When I was a little girl I remember mama telling me that my hair would be nappy and matted on my head if I didn't tie it up in a scarf at night. Thank goodness I learned to do that once I got to junior high school, because this is exactly the way this woman's hair looked.

The young woman watched me like a cat watches a rat he is going to catch for his dinner. As I walked up the stairs to let myself in the building she jumped in front of me. She pressed her face close to my ear. I could feel and smell her hot stinking breath as she whispered menacingly into my ear, "Open this goddamned door quick bitch. You better

not scream or I will run this knife right through your side."
I fumbled in my purse for my key. I tried to keep as still
as possible because I could feel the knife pricking my skin
every time I moved. I finally found the key and my hand
was trembling so badly that I could barely turn the lock.
"You better hurry up bitch if you don't want to die." Once
I got the door opened the woman pushed me to the floor.
She went straight to the cabinets and rambled through the
vaccine bottles and other medicines that had been set aside
for the research project. "You better not try anything." She
yelled to me while she rambled through the cabinets, She
cursed and threw bottles on the floor as she pillaged through
every cabinet in the office. She finally found what she was
looking for. She headed towards the door, turned back,
came to where I was lying on the floor, leaned close to me
and yelled in my face, "You better not call the sheriff bitch,
or I will come back, and find you, and kill your fuckin ass."

I stayed on the floor sobbing hysterically for what seemed
like hours. Finally, my research partner came in and found
me. "Annie she called to me as she ran and knelt beside me.
Oh my goodness, what happened?" I tried through sobs to
explain but I couldn't make my words coherent. "Just lie
still." She said, "I will call the sheriff."

The sheriff came about half an hour later. Maurva,
T-Bo, Mark, and the children had all gotten there by then.
I sat in the chair behind my desk and recanted the horrors
that had happened that morning. We all went home. I went
to bed and had horrible dreams of my brother Willie Earl,
Big Frank, and Lola's daddy all rolled into one.

The sheriff came by the research office a week later and asked me to come down and see a line-up of possible suspects. My whole family came with me. It was easy to spot the girl in the line up. She had the same nappy hair and she had not changed hr clothes. She was still scratching herself. I told the sheriff which one she was. They told me that they would notify me when they needed me.

I received a letter from the sheriff's department stating that the woman had been charged with multiple crimes. They had found her guilty of the other charges; therefore my services would no longer be needed. I was happy to sign the paper and return it in the enclosed envelope. My research partner told me that some painkillers and methamphetamines were taken from the cabinets. The thief had cleaned them out.

Other than the robbery every thing else went smoothly with the research. The women came in, gave their blood and urine samples, and received their treatment. A few of the girls were from the university, but every thing in the clinic was confidential and never to be discussed outside of the walls of the clinic.

Mark and I rarely saw each other these days we were both so busy with classes, internships, research, and work that there was barely time to eat and sleep. We managed to make it through the semester. Christmas was just a blur. We were all so busy with the new baby, classes and work that we barely got to church on Christmas day.

We were eating Christmas dinner when we heard the front door open and someone yelled out is this where Maurva and T-Bo live. It was Bailey! Bailey looked great! His wife and children all came in and we all hugged and kissed, and sat down to our Christmas dinner. It was a wonderful day filled with family, friends, and fun.

Chapter 6

J ANUARY CAME IN cold and windy. We huddled around
the registration building waiting our turn to register
for the spring semester. It didn't seem much like spring
with the way the wind was howling. Mark was registering
for classes and graduation in May. With my accelerated
classes and my research I would be eligible for graduation
in December. Mark and I had worked very hard and taken
extra classes every semester, which made us both eligible for
early graduation.

Mark and I hurried back to the dorm. He would be
back at the bookkeeping office fulltime now. His internship
was almost over. His hours had been cut to 2 day because
of the progress he made with his crop study project. I was
still in full swing with my research at the clinic. We had
more clients than the two of us could handle. I discussed
the situation with Dr. Morgan. He was reluctant to give us
another worker. We invited him to come to the clinic and
watch us work.

We all came in early the next morning. One of the biggest breakthroughs of our work was waiting in our lab in a test tube in the backroom. When Tony, and Adele, got to the lab I was putting my key in the door. I know that we had been warned by the sheriff to wait in our cars and go in the lab as a group but I was anxious to see our results. Monday morning was our busiest time. We usually had more clients on Monday than we had during the whole week. Dr Morgan watched us work from inside of the office with the two-way mirror. "Well ladies" he said when we sat down for lunch in the backroom. My research partner had hung the closed for lunch sign outside the front door when our last morning patient left. "Seems like you could use an assistant. I don't know where we will get the money but you two need an additional pair of hands to complete this job. You have twelve more weeks of tedious work to complete. We expect this work to make a profound impact on venereal disease, Tuskegee, and the world." Dr. Morgan said with pride.

We all rushed to the back room and put our lab coats, gloves, and goggles on. I was first to enter the room. I could see the color change in the tubes from across the room. That was a good sign. Tony took the tubes out of the tube stand slowly as if he was afraid he would spill the contents. We mixed the tube liquids with the samples in the dishes. We covered the dishes and left the room quickly.

We knew that we had to wait at least thirty minutes before we could see if the serum worked on the live samples. We tried to busy ourselves with paper work while we waited.

The half hour dragged on. We prepared the lab for the first clients of the day while we waited.

The half hour dragged by like syrup poured from a bottle. This time we walked into the backroom slowly. We put our goggles and lab coats on and went to the counter for a look. "Look" Adele shouted. "It green with foam." Tony said. "Oh my." I said. We held hands and jumped for joy. "We did it! I shouted. "We did it," I said again and again.

We finished up our reports. Our research was done. We had accomplished our goal. The break through had happened. The research would be fully funded for the next 5 years. We were well on our way to putting venereal diseases under control. We finished up our work, our reports, and packed the samples in shipping cases to be sent to Philadelphia. The final research would be completed there.

Dr. Morgan came by. He was ecstatic. "What can I say? I must tell you that I never thought that it would happen. We have accomplished something here today that I never thought would happen. The first leg for the cure of venereal disease has happened right here. I am so pleased with your work. Each of you will receive a stipend for your work and research here at Tuskegee. Congratulations." Dr. Morgan said with a voice filled with emotion. He took his coat, and umbrella and walked to his car.

We had three weeks to finish the treatment cycle for our patients. We explained to them that our research would be done at the end of the month, and their records would be transferred to the hospital.

Adele, Tony, Dr. Morgan and I went out to dinner on Friday night. We had a great time at "Mama's Soul Food Kitchen." We laughed and talked about our times at Tuskegee, and our research. We discussed our plans for the future, and how we would accomplish them. The stipends had been very generous. I had received $300 and Tony and Adele had each received $150. We were all very pleased.

We left the restaurant and promised to stay in touch. Tony and Adele would be graduating in May. My graduation would not be until December. It was a wonderful evening, with new friends and fond memories for all of us.

Chapter 7

MARK HAD DONE so well with his internship that he had been offered a job. The job was in Dothan, Alabama. He would have to start immediately following graduation. We had a lot to talk over. "Baby do you want to go?" Mark asked. "Of course I do. I want to go wherever you go. I love you Mark." I said as I kissed him. We sat on the porch at the back of my house and tried to work out some details. I had a big thick notebook now. I kept it with me all of the time, because it was filled with all of the things we had to do for both of our graduations and the wedding.

Maurva came out on the porch with ice tea for us. We drank the tea and continued to plan late into the evening. We decided that Mark would graduate and go on to Dothan and start his job. I would stay in Tuskegee and graduate in December. We planned the engagement party for June of next year, and the wedding for August.

The time flew by. It was sunny and hot. The auditorium was filled with people. Mark looked so handsome in his navy blue suit. He waited until just before the ceremony to put on his cap and gown. When they called Mark's name I clapped as loudly as I could with my white gloves, and pink dress. My sorority sisters were seated with me in the auditorium. We all clapped as Mark crossed the stage.

Mark had decided at the last minute to participate in the ceremony. No one in his family had come. T-Bo and Maurva came with me to the ceremony. After the graduation we had dinner at the house. We sat in the living room and talked about our plans with T-Bo and Maurva. They were paying for the reception. Maurva had already asked the best caterer in Madison County Georgia to cater the reception. Miss Hattie had said yes. Maurva said that Miss Hattie had some other ladies working with her now and they were happy to do the reception, for a small fee. Mark said that he would be paying for the rehearsal dinner. "I know that you folks want to help Annie and me but I want to do my share." Mark said adamantly. They all agreed. Mark left to go back to the dorm to do some more packing. He was due in Dothan at his new job on Monday morning. He was leaving at six in the morning. His new boss had made arrangements for him to stay with a family in Dothan until he found a place of his own

.

Mark and Annie never missed a day communicating with each other. They wrote to each other every day. Annie had made a few trips to Dothan. She and Mark found a tiny little house for them in a place called Headland. Headland was very close to Dothan and it was close to Mark's work. The house had a patch of land in the back." It is just right for a garden." Annie said. " I think that we are going to like it here" Mark said. He picked Annie up and carried her inside. Mark took his jacket off and spread it on the floor. Annie sat down, and Mark snuggled up behind her. Mark kissed her passionately. He explored every inch of Annie's mouth with his mouth. Annie responded back. She kissed him with abandonment. Mark began to caress Annie with his hands while he ravished her with his mouth. His hands masterfully removed her blouse and her bra. Annie didn't know how to resist. Her head said no but her body said yes.

Mark knew that he had to be gentle with Annie. They had never made love before. They came close once in his frat house room but he had stopped when Annie said stop. This time it seemed as though neither of them could stop. Mark ravished Annie's body with his mouth. He tasted every inch of her. She was like a drug of which he could not get enough. He looked into her eyes and he saw love, fear, and desire. Tears began to fall from her eyes. The tears made Mark come to his senses. It took all of his will power to get up from the floor. Annie sat up and held her blouse together with her hands. "Mark, are you okay? " she asked. "Oh baby I am so sorry. I didn't mean to take advantage of you. Please forgive me," Mark begged. "No Mark, it's okay." Mark saw by the look in Annie's eyes that she knew what she wanted. They made love in the middle of the floor of the house he was going to move into soon, and someday bring her to this house as his wife.

Mark slid his arm from under Annie's head. He got up and went to the bathroom and cleaned himself up. Annie was sleeping peacefully on his jacket in the middle of the floor where he had left her after their lovemaking. He went to the porch and lit one of his little cigars. Annie loved the smell of the cigars, he thought to himself as he took a long draw from the cigar. "Mark", Annie called from the house. Mark flicked the remainder of the cigar into the dirt as he answered Annie. "Yes baby, I am right here." Mark said, as he knelt down beside her. There was blood all over the front of Annie's slip. Annie looked down and saw what Mark saw. "Oh my God Annie, are you okay"? He tried to help Annie get up. Annie was calm. She had talked with Maurva, Lola, and Cathy about things that might happen the first time she made love with a man. "It's okay Mark" Annie said calmly, as she gathered her things. "Where is the restroom?" She asked. Mark pointed her towards the bathroom. He found some newspaper and cleaned up what was left of the blood. He threw the papers into the rubbish and started a fire in the big rubbish can in the back yard of the house. He watched the fire and his mind wandered back to when he was in college. Mark had been with lots of girls, but no one like Annie. Annie was different. She was special. She was his and he would never let her go. "Mark." Annie called out from the house. "Where are you?" Mark went to the house, gathered Annie in his arms, and put her in the car. He treated her like a fragile glass doll that neither he nor anyone else should break.

Mark Allen drove back to Dothan with Annie in the crook of his arm. Annie picked up her luggage from the rooming house where Mark had reserved a room for her, and they continued their drive to Tuskegee.

It was late when they got back to Maurva's house. "Are you okay Annie?" Mark asked as he walked her to the door. "Yes, I am fine" Annie said. "Look baby, I am sorry I didn't mean, Annie put her finger up to Mark's lips. "Shh" she said please don't spoil it for us, Mark" Annie kissed him on the cheek and let herself in the house. Mark walked back to his car with a grin on his face.

Annie went into the house with love in her heart for a man that meant the world to her and would soon be her husband. Sleep was sweet that night.

Annie woke up to the smell of bacon and biscuits. "Annie", Maurva called from the kitchen. "Come to breakfast." Annie stumbled out of bed, took her bath and went to breakfast. "How was your trip Annie?' Maurva asked. "Fine", Annie said. Maurva noticed that Annie looked different this morning. There was something about her smile, her demeanor. Maurva couldn't quite put her finger on it but Annie was different. "Well I have got to get to the office. I am doing work for two now that you are on maternity leave," Annie said teasingly to Maurva.

Maurva had taken a year off to take care of her children. She had not regained her strength yet. This was the longest it ever took for her to recover from having a baby. She found herself napping in the afternoons when the children took their naps. The doctor had said that she had lost a lot of blood and it sometimes takes women a year or more to recover from childbirth. He told Maurva that she was a little older this time and that was also a factor to consider.

Maurva had asked for the time off and Mr. Calloway had hesitated at first but had finally consented. He knew that Maurva understood the office better than he did. She was good at handling the employees, scheduling time-off, and breaks, and handling difficult situations. He didn't want to lose her so he gave her the time off. "Take as much time as you need Maurva. Your job will be here when you get back." He said on the day Maurva told him about her maternity leave, and what the doctor had said a month later.

Annie was working hard doing her job and trying to fill in for Maurva. She was finally getting the hang of it. Mr. Calloway hired a new delivery guy to replace Mark Allen. He was a college student. He was nice and friendly, but he never stood around and talked. He was always in and out like a flash. He was from Alabama, and wanted to go to New York when he finished school to study acting. There was a guy waiting for him every afternoon to pick him up because he parked the bicycle out back in the shed when he got off. The people in the office whispered about him. They said he was not right. I ignored them for the most part, and told them that they should mind their own business. His name was Bill. They called him Billy. Billy was always helpful and he would do anything that I asked him to do.

Billy and I went to lunch a few times. He talked a lot and shared his life story with me. He told me about his troubled high school years. I felt so sorry for him. His parents kicked him out when he was sixteen. He came to Tuskegee to live with his aunt. She was paying his way through school with her dead husband's insurance policies.

I was sitting in the Purple Onion with Billy having lunch one afternoon when he looked as if he had seen a ghost. "What's wrong Billy?" I asked. He finally said, "Nothing" and we went on talking and eating lunch. When we got ready to leave Billy gave me the money to pay for his lunch." I have to go." He said and went out of the back door. I went to the counter to pay our bill, and I saw Dr. Morgan sitting at the table that was directly behind us. I spoke politely. Dr. Morgan nodded his head and glared at me strangely. I hurried back to work because I was late.

When I got back to the office Mr. Calloway was at his desk. He called me over. "Annie, Billy Mims just quit. He came in from lunch, gave me this note and walked out of the door. What do you make of it?" Mr. Calloway asked with concern. "I don't know Mr. Calloway. We were having lunch and all of a sudden he bolted out of the door." I said hoping that I hadn't said anything to upset him, as some of the others in the office had done for the past two weeks. "Well let's start looking around for another delivery guy," Mr. Calloway said as he walked away shaking his head.

December came around fast. Maurva sent out several invitations to my graduation. The big day finally came. We were all packed in Maurva and T-Bo's house. There were people from Madison County that had come with Mama and Auntie Chauncey. Lola and her whole family had come for the ceremony. Everyone had come for my graduation.

Mark had gotten a new camera and was lining up everyone for pictures. We left for the auditorium in separate cars. It had started to rain and people were moving quickly into the auditorium. Mark had asked one of his fraternity brothers to take a picture of us before I had to line up. He snapped us kissing. I got in line. Mark kissed me and wished me luck.

The scholarships and honors were announced. I sat there fiddling with my pearls, when I thought I heard my name. "Miss Annie Harris, Please come forward." the voice said again. I stood up. My knees were shaking. I went to the stage in a blur. I could hear the applause and I thought that I was going to faint. I walked up to the podium. Dr. Morgan was there holding out his hand. He had a silver object in the other hand. He shook my hand. Dr. Morgan spoke into the microphone. "Ladies and gentlemen it gives me great pleasure to present the Abraham C. Morgan Distinctive Services Award to Miss Annie Harris for outstanding work in the field of biology and research in infectious diseases." Dr. Morgan turned to face me. He said " Miss Harris, congratulations." I could hear the thunderous applause. I stood there and cried. Someone came and led me back to my seat. I sat down and thanked God for my very good fortune. In my heart of hearts I knew that this award belonged to my friend Cathy Lawson who had nearly lost her life for what she thought was true love for her work and another human being.

We all sat around the kitchen table at Maurva's house. We had a good meal and everyone had a good time. The kids all fell asleep and the adults sat around and talked about old times, and good friends. Mama came in the kitchen where we were washing dishes. Maurva was sitting at the table drying dishes because she was tire from standing and cooking all weekend. Mama kissed me and gave me a little box. "Oh mama, thank you so much." Oh baby it's not much but it's from my heart." I opened the box. Inside of the box was an odd object. It looked like a bracelet. It was made of bottle caps that had been flattened and smoothed out and placed on a gold chain. "Mama where did you get this?" Mama was crying. Through her tears she managed to say that Willie Earl had been working on it the year he died. He was making it for your Christmas present. Mr. Curtis finished it for me. He sends his love to you. "Oh mama, I love you. I love Willie Earl. I love everybody who has been a friend to me.

Chapter 8

MARK GATHERED EVERYONE into the backyard. The house had become filled with family and friends. Mark wanted everyone to hear what he had to say. "I am so happy to be here with all of you today on this wonderful, joyful occasion. I am preparing to marry one of the beautiful people in this family. Come on up here baby." Mark said as the crowd applauded. Annie walked up and stood by Mark's side. She kissed him on the cheek and the crowd roared with laughter, and applause. " I, we, Annie and me have something we need to share with you. Bea Harris sat down in the green swing and Auntie Chauncey massaged her shoulders. Mark had already discussed with them about finding the sack but that was all. He didn't tell them the rest of his plan.

Annie called Lola up to stand with them. Annie and Lola told the story that had haunted them over 15 years. As the two women told the story tears flowed from their eyes. Annie told about her promise to her dead brother

Willie Earl, and how she had kept it all these years. She told about the letters she found behind the cupboard that told about her father's other life with Miss Francine. The women shared about the baby that Miss Viola had raised under the direction and financial benefits of Miss Hattie and Miss Francine. When they finished everyone was crying and many of them were in shock.

Mark took the sack from his jacket and emptied the contents on the table. There was a stack of money, papers, and a brown envelope. Mark handed the money to T-Bo to count. There was a birth certificate for a child. The birth certificate stated that a colored boy was born to Francine Rittenberry a white woman, 21 years old. The brown envelope was last to be opened. It contained a marriage certificate, and military papers. The marriage certificate was for Clarence Harris and Francine Rittenberry. They were married on a military base in Hawaii. There was a note in the bag explaining about the money. The money in the sack was for the Harris family for all of the trouble brought on them by Dial Harris and Francine Rooker. Mama fainted on the porch, and Auntie Chauncey screamed and ran into the house. She came back with an ice pack for mama's head. You could hear a pin fall in that yard.

T-Bo handed the money back to Mark. Mark put the money back in the sack along with the other papers. Annie and Lola went back to the porch. Mark continued with his story. "We have brought this to your attention because we want this matter to be put to rest. After tonight there will be no further discussion of this matter." Mark said distinctly.

T-Bo spoke up. " I counted $10,000. I believe that the money should go to Annie. Annie is just starting out and she will need the money." Everyone applauded loudly and shouted yes and amen.

The crowd finally thinned out. Everyone went to their own home. Annie and Mark checked on mama and Auntie Chauncey. Mama was still shaking from the news. I hugged her. "Mama I hope that you are as happy as I am to finally have everything settled. I know that it was a bit of a shock to hear all of those things but daddy is dead, and everything is not important anymore. I can put my brother's struggle to keep us all from shame to rest now. It's okay now mama." I said as I wiped her face with a cloth from the table. We can all move forward now, without the dead weight and ghost of times past holding us back." I said as Mark knelt down and embraced us all in his big strong arms. I felt safe and protected from all of the terrors of the world in the arms of my lover and my friend.

Chapter 9

The Engagement Party

S WEETIE BELL WINSTON Allen was a force to be reckoned with when she was planning an event. She was chairwoman of the Women's Negro League, President of her sorority, Delta Sigma Theta, director of the Debutante Cotillion, and advisor to the President of the NAACP. She had planned events and parties since she was twenty-one. She was the creator of the Negro Social Registry for her district, and she barred anyone that crossed her, no matter how much money they had or what their pedigree was. Sweetie Bell was a Southern Negro belle, and a snob. No one liked her, but everyone obeyed her. If Sweetie said jump they jumped, no matter how high.

The hall had been rented. The caterer had been hired, and the help had been thoroughly screened. The Negro Country club had cancelled all events for the week leading up to the engagement party. Sweetie personally inspected every uniform that every server and attendant would be wearing. She made sure that the cooks used premium quality pork and beef. Sweetie personally inspected the toilets herself. The liquor was left to her husband's discretion. Sweetie was a teetotaler. But her husband knew every brand of liquor west of the Mississippi. He could carry his liquor well. He had personally ordered all of the liquor, beer and wine for the party. He also had a secret stash of White Lighting, (better known as moonshine) for his friends that liked a little home brew like himself. Of course he kept that from Sweetie. She would have his head on a platter if she ever found out he had the White Lighting anywhere near the party.

The room was gorgeous. It was covered in greenery with red roses and white ribbons. It didn't matter that Annie was an AKA, this was Sweetie's affair and many of the people attending would make a Greek smorgasbord, and Sweetie had to represent Delta in a big way. There were red roses everywhere. There were red and white placemats, tiny umbrellas, and napkins that said Mark and Annie 1963.

The floor was covered with artificial red flowers. White streamers dangled from the crystal chandeliers. There were tiny Christmas lights strung around tiny evergreen trees. The tables were covered with white linen cloths. Red linen napkins and finger bowls with red water graced each table. A tall candelabrum was in the middle of each round table. The long tables in the front of the room were covered with every type of food imaginable.

There were tables with seafood, lobster, roast beef, ribs, chicken, rolls, desserts, pastries, vegetables, and pasta. The beverages were at a long bar attended by two bartenders wearing white waistcoats and red vest. The champagne fountain flowed freely during the entire party.

The hostesses wore white uniforms with red aprons. The servers wore white jackets with red napkins draped over their arms. Sweetie had everyone lined up against the country club wall for inspection an hour before the event. When everything was to her satisfaction the doors were opened to the guest. Some of them had been waiting an hour in the hot sun. No one in Mississippi wanted to miss a Sweetie Bell Winston Allen affair.

Sweetie had hired Sonny Brown and his band Renowned to play for the party. She had insisted that they wear tuxedoes with red cummerbunds. She and Sonny got into a big argument but they finally came to an agreement Sweetie had to pay for the rental of the tuxedos for every band member and Sonny. Sweetie Bell paid for the rental, but Sonny and his band agreed to play two hours for free. Sweetie always got her way. No matter the cost.

Her daddy had made enough money running bootleg whiskey and taking care of sick black folks to let Sweetie live in style. The insurance money from her mother's death was enough to help support her lavish lifestyle. Her daddy, old doc Winston had passed for white for many years and had received pay like a white doctor for all those years. He had worked in the white hospital in Tupelo for many years without being discovered. He had learned to invest money early on by listening to white people talk. Winston had made some shrewd investments that had paid off well. Now his daughter could spend money freely without fear of ever being in lack.

Sweetie had chosen to wear a long red gown covered in sequins. Her husband had a new tuxedo with a red brocade cummerbund. The guest arrived in droves. One hundred and fifty people had been invited. Everyone accepted the invitations that Sweetie Bell sent out. The hall was filled with people from Mississippi Alabama, New York, and Georgia. All of Annie's family and friends were there. Her mother, brothers, auntie, sister, brother and sisters –in law had all arrived and were seated in the front across from Mark's family. Annie and Mark were the only one's missing.

Mark sat on the bed with his head in his hands and told Annie that he was too sick to go. Annie knew that Mark wasn't sick physically. He could not be in the same room with his mother for more than five minutes before an argument started. "Mark", Annie cooed. Try it for me. We don't have to stay long. We will make an appearance and have dinner and leave. It won't be so bad. We can do it together." Mark got up from the bed, looked into Annie's beautiful brown eyes and he melted like butter. Annie mesmerized Mark. It was like she had a spell over him. He loved her more than life itself, and it showed in everything he did that involved her. "Okay baby I will do it just for you." Mark knew that he would have to stay far away from his mother to make it through the evening.

When Mark and Annie entered the room they were both shocked at the entire gala. They had planned on a small engagement party, but Mark's mom had other ideas, and everyone always let her have her way. "What did I tell you Annie?" Mark moaned. Everything with my mother is always way out. I mean way out." Mark said as he stretched his arms wide. "It's okay Mark. Let's just get through it. It will be okay," Annie said as she held on tightly to Mark's arm.

As Mark and Annie entered the room the announcer asked everyone to stand and receive the engaged couple. Mr. Mark Allen, and Miss Annie Harris, let's give them a rousing round of applause as they lead us in our first dance of the evening. Mark was a smooth dancer and led Annie gracefully around the floor.

The guest danced to Sonny Brown's jazz, blues, and soulful strut. They did the twist, the jerk, the two-step, and everything that Sonny played music for. As the evening drew to a close the couples paired off for the last slow dance of the evening.

Mark and Annie slow danced onto the veranda. The night air was cool. The stars were shining brightly, and the moon had a halo around it. "Glad you came?" Annie asked? as she smiled up into Mark's eyes. "I am happy anywhere that you and I are together." Mark said romantically. "I love you so much Annie. Will you marry me?" Annie knew that Mark was going to ask her, and she had always practiced what she would say. "I, I, ah, yes Mark, yes I will marry you. Tears rolled down her cheeks as she tried to compose myself. Mark took the little black box that he kept with him at all times from his tuxedo pocket, got down on one knee and asked Annie again; "Annie will you be my wife? "Oh Mark, yes, yes, a thousand times yes.

I got back to Tuskegee just in time to change my clothes and get to my bridal shower. My sorority sisters were giving me a shower at Mrs. Betty Morgan's house. I had met Mrs. Morgan once at the driver's license bureau. She had been very reluctant to tell me her name. She had loaned Mark and me the money we needed to get my driver's license. She wouldn't give us her address so we had no way of sending her the money to pay her back.

When I arrived at 304 Washington Street, around the lake, I was met outside by a group of ladies that wrapped me in pink ribbon and bows. When I got inside I saw beautifully wrapped packages of all shapes and sizes. There were pretty pink napkins, tiny green sandwiches, punch bowls, filled with pink and green punch, and lettuce leaves stuffed with pimento cheese.

I opened gifts and tried out sweepers, and twirled around mops with a vengeance. We had so much fun with the gifts. We were like kids on Christmas morning. The girls helped me pack everything into the car. I drove myself home. I could barely see because the car was packed with gifts.

T-Bo and the kids helped me unpack the car. Maurva was inside lying down. Since this last baby she had not come back to herself yet. She still got very tired easily and quickly. I tried staying close to home just in case she needed me. Time was getting close for the wedding and things were more hectic than usual. I tried to be very considerate of Maurva and her condition.

The ladies from our church in Tuskegee and the ladies from Live Oak Baptist church got together and gave me a Boudoir Shower. There were flannel nightgowns, lingerie, housecoats, and bed jackets, plenty of fancy underwear, and things that were indescribable. We had fun with all of the fancy gifts.

It took me three days to finish writing thank-you notes. I got Maurva to help me. It was a big job, but together Maurva and I got it done.

Chapter 10

The Wedding

IT WAS A beautiful summer morning. I walked back from the church after one final peek at the sanctuary and the fellowship hall. The sanctuary was filled with greenery trimmed with pink bows and mint green ribbons. There were tall candelabras with pink candles underneath the glass with pink streamers hanging down each side of the glass. They were place at the entryway on either side of the foyer. Each window had greenery around the sill and pink streamers. There were pink and white bows on each pew with a sprig of baby breath tucked into each bow. Five streamers of pink ribbon were looped through each ceiling light fixture. The wedding arch was also trimmed with green flowers and tiny pink artificial roses. There was a kneeling bench covered with white satin. There were green plants placed all around the sanctuary. The plants were sitting on little white stands that were trimmed with tiny pink ribbons. It was the most beautiful sight I had ever seen in my life.

The fellowship hall was full of long tables covered with white cloths. Each table had pink and green runners down the center. There were small glass candelabra on each table. The candles were pink and white with pink ribbons on each candle. Each chair was covered with pink cloth and wrapped with a satin bow. There were six punch bowls donated by Mr. Curtis' customers at the barbershop. The cake was eighteen inches tall. It was covered with pink and white icing and covered with tiny pink roses all around the edges of the six layers. Miss Hattie had baked the cake just for my wedding. She had come from Georgia and stayed with Rev and Mrs. Tremble the whole week and worked on it. It was beautiful. Mama had made the two people on the top. She had made them from straw and cloth. They looked so cute.

I walked back to the sanctuary and I stood there in the sanctuary and cried. I cried for all of the happy and unhappy memories that the Live Oak Baptist Church held for me. It was a scene from a storybook, and one that I would never forget as long as I lived. My mind wondered back to the day of the funeral of my brother, Willie Earl. It was a sad and tragic event, that has haunted me all of my life. My mind went back to the wedding of my first grade teacher Miss Sutton. I was little girl with the big job of flower girl. The years had passed quickly. Now, Mrs. Sutton-Solomon was my soro, and in charge of my wedding.

We were all gathered together in the house on Merritt Street. Sammy and Pearline and their children had driven all the way from North Carolina. Sammy was stationed there now. He was a Captain in the army. He was still very handsome, and neatly dressed. His frame was full and fit. Pearline had put on a little weight but she was still very pretty. Bailey and his wife and children came in his new truck. It was a green with a black cab on the back. When Bailey walked in with his family he looked so proud.

Sammy and Bailey still had to get dressed. They were in the wedding party. They both had black tuxedos, and would serve as ushers. Mark's fraternity brothers were going to serve as groomsmen. His daddy was his best man.

The bridesmaid's dresses were beautiful. They were cream-colored after-fives with pink shawls that wrapped around the top half of the dress with a mint green insert. They each had a halo of baby breath to wear in their hair. Maurva's baby girl, Bailey's baby girl, and Sammy's daughter were flower girls. Their dresses were white with pink flowers sprinkled all through the pink net overlay. The two little boys were bell ringer and ring bearer.

Before going on to the church Mark's mom and dad came in the door just to say hello. They were staying at Auntie Chauncey's house, along with Mark, Bailey, and his family. Mark's dad was driving a black Cadillac with silver chrome. It was a beautiful car. Mark's mom was dressed in a pale pink chiffon dress with silver shoes. She had her hair pulled back in a French twist, with tiny little flowers stuck in the twist. Her hat was perched high on top of her head and the brim was lowered over one eye. She looked beautiful. His dad had a black tuxedo with a shiny black cumber bund and black patent leather shoes. His shirt was a pale pink. His hair was silver and parted on the side. He was handsome in a rugged sort of way. I knew from looking at Mark's daddy what Mark would look like when he got older.

Maurva and T-Bo and the children changed into their wedding clothes. Maurva's after-five dress was pink with a cream colored and mint green insert. Maurva and Lola were going to stand up with me. Lola and her husband came in the back door. Jackson was wearing his army uniform. He had to leave as soon as the ceremony was over. Lola was going to stay with her mother, brothers and sisters. Cathy had made it to the wedding. I didn't think that she would make it but she was there with a great big smile on her face. She looked great! She was with a young man that seemed to hang on her every word. He was very handsome and had a funny accent. Cathy said he was from East St Louis, and that was how they talked. Cathy Lawson was dressed in a pink and green chiffon after-five with sequins sprinkled throughout the bodice. All of the bridesmaids had pink bows with short-laced veils that stopped at the brim of the nose

I sat on the couch and watched all of my family and friends rush around trying to get things ready for my wedding. Nearly every person in the Live Oak Baptist church had contributed something to this wedding. Mrs. Tremble had done all of the flowers. Mrs. Solomon had decorated the church. It was full of beautiful green ferns and pink flowers.

There was pink netting draped over everything that was standing. There was an arch covered with pink and green flowers. Miss Francine had sent the candelabra and arch over from the funeral home in South Carolina.

I went to the bedroom and started to get dressed. I sat down on the footstool where I got my hair pressed every weekend. I thought about my brother Willie Earl and I cried because I missed my brother. He was only fourteen when he was murdered. Mama came in and helped me finish getting dressed. We got the hoop slip on first. Then we slid the dress over my head. I had to have three fittings because I kept losing weight. We finally got it right. Mama fastened the pearls that Mrs. Solomon, my first grade teacher, who was also my sorority sister, had given me.

My dress must have a thousand buttons down the back Mama. I said impatiently as mama buttoned each button on the dress. The dress was covered in white lace with clusters of beads in little sections on the bodice. The hoop made the dress stand out at least what seemed to like 10 yards. The bottom was covered in Chantilly lace. The bodice was fitted and had a tiny bow at the base of the back. The train was at least 3 feet long. It was decorated with tiny pink and white roses. The sleeves were capped and each sleeve was covered in Chantilly lace.

I was getting ready to put on my pumps when mama pulled a box from under the bed. The box had a pair of the most beautiful shoes I had ever seen. "I bet you will never guess where I got these shoes," mama said with a twinkle in her eyes. "Where mama?" I asked anxiously. Mama sat on the stool beside the bed and told me where the shoes came from. "Well you remember Mr. Neuman don't you baby?" Mama asked. "Yes ma'am." I said. Mr. Neuman has passed on but his son, young Mr. Neuman took over the store. When you and Mark came down to visit last year Mark and Mr. Curtis went shopping in the store. It seems that Mark saw a catalog in the store and started thumbing through it while he waited for his packages. He saw the shoes and asked Neuman to order them for him. Mark paid for the shoes that day. Well here they are." The shoes were white and covered with beads and rhinestones. They matched perfectly with my dress. There was an insert in each shoe. The writing was beautifully done. The letters were AAH . I put the shoes on my feet and I felt like Cinderella. They fit perfectly.

The initials were for Annie Harris Allen. I knew why it was written with my new last name in the middle because when I crossed over my sorority sisters had given me lots of gifts. A few of my sorority sisters were already married and they explained to me that when you got married your married initial becomes your middle initial but only in embroidery on gifts. All other times your maiden name becomes your middle initial and your new married name is your last name. It was hard to understand but it was making sense now. I loved my shoes and the man who gave them to me. "Let's hurry baby. We have got to get to the church. I gathered my things and hurried out of the door with mama.

It was hot, and my dress was making me even hotter. When I looked up from watching my steps while coming down from the porch, I saw one of the biggest and longest cars I had ever seen. It was black and shining like a new penny. A man got out of the driver's side and came and took my arm. He opened the door and put me, and all of my dress in the back seat. The car was nice and frosty. The man went back to the porch to get mama, who was standing on the porch in a "trance." He put mama in the front seat. We drove the short distance to the church. We drove around back and went through the Sunday school department so that no one would see me.

I could feel the cold air swirling around the room. The church's new air conditioning system was working full speed. I stood there letting the cool air go through me. Mama took the powder sponge from her purse and rubbed it across my face. That powder sponge was as old as I was, and it looked it. I had never used make-up before so I wasn't about to try it now. Mama smoothed my hair back up on my head. I had ringlets of swirl curls all over my head. My veil was attached to a pearl tiara. Mama put some pale pink lipstick on my lips. It looked very pretty.

There was a knock on the door. "Ladies it's time, a voice said through the door. Please come out. We went into the hall. I caught a glimpse of myself in the same mirror that I looked in as a little girl in Miss Sutton's wedding. Just like then, I didn't recognize myself.

I stood in the church foyer and waited for the usher to come for me. I had not asked anyone to walk me down the aisle. I had decided to walk alone. As I stood there with Lola and Maurva Jean standing in front of me waiting to enter the church I thought about daddy and how much I loved him. In spite of all of the things he had done my heart was still overruling my head. Maurva, and then Lola walked into the sanctuary. The doors closed behind them. Mrs. Sutton-Solomon adjusted my veil and kissed me on my cheek." Good luck, soro, I hope that you will be as happy as I am. I speak blessings over you." As I picked up the front of my gown and was preparing to walk into the church sanctuary T-Bo and Sammy came through the doors from the sanctuary. They stood on either side of me and took my arms into the crook of theirs.

I heard the organ music as it played Here Comes the Bride. Sammy looked at me and said, "I love you baby sister. T-Bo kissed my cheek and said, "That's goes double for me." Mrs. Solomon opened the doors and we stepped forward. Everyone in the Live Oak Baptist Church was standing and looking at me. I walked into the church and down the aisle. I saw all of my old friends and neighbors.

I walked to the front of the church and Rev. Tremble looked at me and smiled. He asked: "Who gives this woman in marriage? T-Bo and Sammy said, "We do." They each kissed me on the cheek and sat down. Mark looked so handsome. His face and eyes were glowing. The next thing I knew Rev. Tremble was saying, "You may kiss the bride.

We enjoyed the food that had been prepared for us. We greeted friends, and family, and took lots of pictures. We went outside to toss the bouquet. I aimed high and pitched the bouquet over my head. That is all that I remember.

When I came too Mama was rubbing my face with a cool cloth. "Oh mama, what happened?" I asked. "Oh you got a little too hot baby and with all this running around, it's no wonder you passed out." Mama cooed. "Mark, where is Mark?" I asked frantically. "Hey baby. You okay?" Mark asked as he took me in his arms. "Yes," I murmured. Mark turned his head to my face and pressed his lips close to my ear and whispered, "For a minute or two I thought that I had lost my best friend. I love you forever Annie," Mark Allen said as we snuggled together in the fainting room of the Live Oak Baptist Church in Madison County, Georgia.

About the Author

BETTY MARSHALL WAS born and raised in Atlanta, Georgia. As a child she loved reading, writing, and acting. She was always encouraged by her friends to put her talents on paper so that many people could enjoy her work. She has authored numerous, plays and skits. Most of her work has been used to entertain religious audiences in churches across the country. Betty resides in Alabama, and is the mother of one daughter and surrogate mother to hundreds of children throughout the United States. She loves animals, and draws much of her material for writing from the people she encounters in life. "I love to laugh and to make others laugh. A merry heart does a body good."